The House of Rats

"Help!" cried Esther, tilting back her head to throw her voice up the grey rise of balconies, windows and snowy ledges. Carl, Zachary, and even Frankie, instantly joined in her cry.

Zachary's voice suddenly acquired a new urgency. "Quiet! All of you! Look!"

He pointed.

Despite the wind, something had indeed heard – a wolf. Starved and ragged, it stood black and still.

The children scrambled back into the parlour and out of the wind. They attacked the heavy door again. Glancing back, as if through smoke, they saw not one wolf, but four. All at once, a baying pack of wolves was careering through the drifts, in an arc that grew ever more well-defined as it closed in on that snowy room.

Then they heard a voice.

The House of Rats

Stephen Elboz

Lions
An Imprint of HarperCollins*Publishers*

First published in Great Britain by Oxford University Press 1991
First published in Lions 1994
3 5 7 9 10 8 6 4 2

Lions is an imprint of the Children's Division,
part of HarperCollins Publishers Ltd,
77–85 Fulham Palace Road,
Hammersmith, London W6 8JB

Copyright © Stephen Elboz 1991

The author asserts the moral right to
be identified as the author of this work

ISBN 0 00 674812-0

Set in Plantin
Printed and bound in Great Britain by
HarperCollins Manufacturing, Glasgow

For Mum and Dad

Esther's Prologue

One damp foggy morning, the man who called himself "the Master" threw down his napkin and strode out from the big house, never to return.

(Some remembered seeing him thrust a letter into his pocket. But so much was later added to the truth.)

Of course the servants went searching for him. Through one of the grimy attic windows we looked down at the dense ragged forest, listening to their shouts. Glimpsing their lanterns through the trees. When they returned, without him, they gathered below us, shaking their heads and discussing the various easy ways a man could lose his life in the forest.

None of us cried. We were not even sad. We were more puzzled. How could he – the master – break our daily routine? This man who ran the big house to a published timetable? Who was known to dismiss a servant for a minute's lateness? Who had a clock in every room – sometimes whole banks of them, their pendulums swinging in silent unison?

For a while the timetable became its own master. Zachary, Frankie, Carl and myself went to our lessons, sharing the same dreary schoolroom and teacher, Miss Frost; even though Zachary and I are four years older than Carl, and Frankie, who is simple, played with bricks all day long on the schoolroom floor.

I remember, a few days after the master disappeared, it was geography.

"Save for its mountains and gulleys," said Miss Frost, pointing at an ancient map of the world, "the Earth is quite flat. At either end lies a thunderous waterfall. T-H-U-N-D-E-R-U-S-S. Thunderous, my dear children. Pity the poor unfortunate mariner on his way to the New World or Cathay, who plunges into the dreadful abyss. A speck in the deluge, dear children. A speck."

I imagined the master being swept away across an ocean and over a roaring waterfall. *A speck in the deluge*. I saw his sad, pale face as the foam broke over his little boat . . .

That evening Dunn, the butler, served dinner. He appeared in his bowler hat (the usual beads of sweat just under its brim) and immaculately white gloves. The master's place was set. When his soup grew a skin, Dunn took it away. We ate our roast chicken in silence, wondering whether to ask Dunn for his advice. But to do this we would have to admit that the master was gone for ever, and the hold of the timetable was too strong for that. We half believed the master was testing us. Watching us through the walls; his dark eyes blinking through those frightening portraits that lined the dim corridors.

So slowly and silently we ate our dinner, chewing every mouthful thirty-seven times, as was the rule, and went to bed at half past eight on the dot.

On the way to our schoolroom the next morning, Zachary let out a gasp.

"What's wrong?" I asked.

"Look!" he said, pointing at a shelf. There was a clock, like a golden egg on the back of a gilded elephant. It had stopped.

"Probably broken," I said, as Zachary took it down, and he and Carl removed the back. The key was inside.

"Hey, it hasn't been wound up!" cried Carl indignantly. He turned the key until it would turn no more and set it back on the shelf. Stopping to wind the clock made us ninety seconds late, so we hurried to our classroom and Miss Frost.

Another surprise was in store for us as we entered. Miss Frost, usually dressed in sensible greys or browns, was wearing a long purple dress, a white frilly blouse and, carelessly cast about her shoulders, an old fox fur. Its eyes were of glass.

"Ah, good morning, children," she said, as brightly as those eyes.

It struck nine just as we were sitting down. As one we lifted our desk tops to take out our sum books.

"Do close your desks, dear children," we heard Miss Frost say. "And put away those tiresome books. I thought we'd do something different today . . ."

I looked at Zachary, and could see Carl shifting uneasily. *Different*. Nothing should ever be different.

"You may not be aware, children," continued Miss Frost, "but I am a talented poetess. Previously I have confined my romantic verse to my diary. But today I thought I would share with you my meditations on matters of the heart."

And this she proceeded to do. We sat dumbfounded while she assumed attitudes and voices so ridiculous that even Frankie stopped playing with his bricks and started laughing and clapping his hands.

That evening Dunn arrived two minutes late.

After serving up the soup he excused himself and, moving to a corner, took off his gloves and blew his nose with such a trumpeting that Carl said pointedly he felt sick.

Going to bed, we found one corridor unlit and, once in my bed, I noticed faint powdery dust on my washstand. I blew out my candle at once and lay listening to the rats scratching about in the attic above my room. Some nights they scratch away for hours and hours.

Miss Frost was wearing red stockings when we went to our lessons the next morning. Instead of cosmology she read us extracts from her favourite novel, *The Tall Dark Man*, and sighed a lot. The following day we were even more scandalized to find a man sitting beside her at her desk.

"This is Gorgio," she announced with a giggle. "He is my new assistant."

"Poo!" sneered Carl, who knew he worked in the kitchens.

We stared hard at them over our books. But it was as if we didn't exist. They whispered behind their hands and sniggered at the notes they wrote to each other.

But this was nothing compared to their sickening behaviour later on. Gorgio reached out, stroked Miss Frost's head and, in the same movement, undid her hair, letting it cascade down her back. She, leaning across her desk, licked his ugly nose with the tip of her tongue – as if it were a cherry on a cake!

This sort of thing should not go on in front of young children, especially by people who are paid to educate them.

There wasn't so much as a note to explain their absence in the afternoon, so Zachary read aloud from *Indians of North America*, a favourite book of his. Every page has a hand-painted picture, although I don't care for any of them myself. They frighten me. I remember one particular plate showing the braves out hunting buffalo. Each is disguised in the skin of a wolf, the wolves' heads fitting those of the hunters like caps. The boys like to pore over this picture, talking a great deal about knives and bows and traps. They did so then.

Suddenly Carl jumped up on a desk and shouted excitedly: "Watch me!" And, jumping from desk top to desk top, he bounded to the stock cupboard at the back of the room. Apart from containing some broken pens and dog-eared books, this was where Miss Frost kept her pride and joy – a heavy mink coat that had once belonged to her mother. He pulled it over his head and immediately began stalking about the schoolroom. Then Zachary slipped in behind him, becoming the back part of a four-legged beast that walked with a sinister swagger.

"We are the wolf men," sang Carl in his high, piping voice.

Frankie was on a desk, no doubt copying Carl. He was making the Red Indian whoop, clumsily striking his mouth with a palm.

"If you're not of our tribe, you are an outcast!" declared Zachary from deep within the coat's velvety folds. "And the wolf men will track you down and kill you."

"Esther's not playing our game," said Carl, peering from the coat and grinning wickedly. "She must be our enemy."

"Stop it," I said, trying to sound braver than I felt. "Stop it at once. Miss Frost may come back at any moment and catch you in her coat."

"Hunt Esther – Hunt Esther!" the boys were chanting, with Frankie banging a desk top. "Hunt Esther – Hunt Esther!" And the thing that was part human and part animal was slowly swaggering across the room towards me. I was shaking with fear, even though I knew it was only the boys.

"Hunt Esther – Hunt Esther!" They kept on saying it, over and over again.

It was then that I screamed. A piercing terrified scream. The boys stood gazing at me in bewilderment, the coat a crumpled heap about their feet. At the door stood Mr Dunn with his hands on his hips.

"It was only a game," explained Carl defensively. "Only a game."

I ran to Mr Dunn and clung to his side, crying and shaking.

"There, there," he said, wiping his hand down my face, collecting tears with his fingers.

"We were just being a wolf," mumbled Carl.

"Well, you shouldn't be scaring people like that, Master Carl. Wolves are not things to be taken lightly."

"Leah the maid says if you invite a wolf into your house it'll become human and turn against you."

"Leah talks rubbish at times."

"So it's not true?" asked Zachary.

Mr Dunn ushered me back to the boys. "Not only is it not true, why, it's plain daft. Who on earth would go inviting a wolf into their home in the first place?"

When he had gone Zachary said darkly, "But wolves are cleverer than you think, Mr Dunn. You can't always see through their disguises." And Carl whooped like an Indian brave.

Chapter One

Wearily, Dunn set off home across the formal gardens. Now he was finished for the day, his bowler hat was tipped at a jauntier angle. Grease blackened the tips of his otherwise immaculate white gloves. He told himself it was the sign of honest toil, and he knew there'd be a clean pair waiting for the morning. Behind him rose the hundred dark towers of the house with their countless empty windows. Around him the gardens lay covered in a light powdering of snow. More will come soon, thought Dunn gloomily, his breath steaming through his muffler.

As he entered the forest's shadow, he paused to hear the clock tower boom the twelve chimes of midnight. Then he turned up his collar and walked quietly on.

Dunn's home was a lodge in the forest. The

track leading there was worn by his own feet (and the occasional passing of his dear wife, Aphid). It wouldn't be long now before the wolves'd be pressing in around the great house, and he would walk armed with a loaded musket and his special umbrella that was also a flame-thrower.

Turning a corner, he saw the curious folly that was his home. All the lights were blazing. It was Aphid, Dunn told himself, they were her lights welcoming him home. A warm fondness for his wife spread through his insides. Lovingly he undid the latch and entered the kitchen.

Aphid was stirring a great cauldron of sheep's heads.

"It's me, dearest," he said softly.

Without turning she made a grunt.

Dunn removed his bowler and gloves. Already the heat of the kitchen was making the sweat beads run. Condensation trickled down the windows.

"Supper smells good. Is it nearly ready, my dear?" asked Dunn, smiling at the back of his wife's head.

Again she made the grunt, but didn't turn around.

Dunn remained smiling, but a mild sense of disappointment came upon him.

"I'll just hang up m'bowler," he said brightly. "Make it look like I'm stopping."

Aphid continued to stir as vigorously as before.

In the oppressive, dimly-lit dining-room, Dunn cast his eyes down a table laid for eight. The other diners were already assembled. Yawning, scratching and sniffing. They didn't come to Dunn. They were Aphid's *boys*. Dunn regretted the fact they had no proper children: resenting Aphid's dogs and the way she dressed them as small boys, in shorts and jumpers.

Just then Aphid marched in carrying a tureen of steaming clay-coloured liquid. She swept past Dunn crying: "Supper time, boys!"

The dogs immediately scrambled to their places.

"Paws off! Paws off! Manners, Bobby!" chided Aphid. She was one of those sinewy women who could never be still. No sooner had she set down the tureen than she was ladling the soup out, slopping it everywhere in her haste.

"Will you be seated, Mr Dunn?" she asked. Now she was hacking at the bread, and rough-cut wedges dropped on to the table.

Dunn seasoned his soup so heavily that the dachshund beside him sneezed.

"Bless you, Tom," said Aphid, not looking up.

She was spooning up her soup, even as she shuffled her chair into position beneath her. The dogs were timorously licking the hot soup at the edges, trying to nip out the meat with their teeth.

Rolling up their lips, they looked ridiculously fierce. Dunn cast his weary gaze along the table then, with a single slurp, drowned out the eating noises of everyone else. As he finished, he was aware that Aphid had just addressed him.

"Er . . . pardon, dearest?"

"I said, how is it up at the house?"

"Bad. Chronically bad. And'll get no better I'd say." Dunn stirred his soup. "I dismissed another three today. Things are so slack, Master'll turn in his gr . . . Master'll be displeased when he gets back."

"Back!" spat Aphid. "I tell you, Dunn, he's never coming back. Everyone else knows this, why don't you? Believe me, others are getting rich on knowing it too. Pockets are bulging – except ours. Them others aren't stupid. Why dust a trinket when you can just as well pick it up and walk off with it? You know what *I* think."

Dunn bowed his head as if he was a naughty child. "But what about the master's youngsters?"

"Them! They're not his. They're foundlings. Charity mites. No more linked by blood to the old master, than to you and me, Dunn. He got them to prettify his table. Forget them, they're worthless."

Aphid snatched up a hunk of break, roughly ripped it apart and cast the pieces down the table. At once her dogs leapt up and wolfed them down.

"Still—"

"Still nothing, Mr Dunn," said Aphid, chewing as she spoke. "Aren't you head man? Haven't you been at the house longer than anyone else? And don't that count for nothing? Besides, Mr Dunn, it isn't a house but a Kingdom and its master a King – and that is your natural due, man. The servants respect you. Not those foundlings, they deserve nothing. They've enjoyed the good life far too long." Aphid's expression softened. "And surely, Mr Dunn, your poor faithful wife deserves her own personal maid by now?"

Dunn picked up his spoon again. She had been badgering him like this since the master disappeared. She had been so cold and off-hand. He stirred his soup, and dislodged something that came floating to the surface. It was a sheep's eye. It stared up at him.

When her husband had risen and gone to work at dawn the following morning, Aphid called up her boys, taking them deep into the forest for their constitutional. The dogs wore little hooded coats, for it was beginning to snow quite heavily.

In a clearing she paused. There, unmarked but quite distinct, was a new grave that couldn't have been much above a fortnight old. Immediately the dogs began to sniff around it. Aphid's complexion turned grey and she drew her mouth tight. Even as she watched, the falling flakes covered over the freshly turned earth.

Chapter Two

It snowed heavily. The children watched through the schoolroom window after making spy-holes in the ice. Snow swirled like smoke. At their backs, schoolbooks lay uselessly strewn across their desks and Frankie had built a brick tower on Miss Frost's stool. As for Miss Frost, they hadn't seen her since last Tuesday, when she had turned up with dyed blonde hair, and a contrasting black eye. After throwing herself across the desk she had sobbed "Gorgio! Gorgio!" several times, then got up and left, her mascara running down her face, as if her eyes were chocolate and she had sat too close to the fire.

"Stuff," murmured Frankie, enchanted by the snow.

"Snow'll bring the wolves," said Zachary.

"Wolfs," mouthed Frankie. "Hungry wolfs."

Esther thought about the snow outside and the dust settling inside the house.

They watched in silence, until Carl said: "I wonder what snow's like to run in?" When the master was in charge, they had been forbidden to play outside throughout the winter months. "I bet it's fun," he said.

Suddenly Zachary elbowed the others aside and threw open the window. In billowed the wind, the snow carried upon it. Leaning out he scooped an armful from the ledge and hauled it into the room. Frankie started to dance around the heap. The others looked down with an exaggerated interest as it began to melt. At once they burst out laughing. They knew that they could not leave the room until every last white speck was water. Zachary glanced at the clock. "We're late for dinner," he grinned.

A mop and bucket had been abandoned outside the dining-room. The children were able to ignore such sights now. Hurrying through the tall double doors, their eyes went automatically to the master's seat, the great high-backed chair at the end of the table. His place was set like any other night – but vacant. The candles guttered violently in the draught until they pushed the doors to. Dunn smiled slightly, and slightly inclined his head. Nobody spoke. That was one of the master's strictest rules which, as yet, remained fully observed.

Dunn served the soup. They began to eat but stopped suddenly and began staring at Dunn. He had removed his bowler and hooked it over the back of the master's chair. Now he was peeling off his gloves. And ... and ... he was actually settling himself in the master's place and lifting a spoon to eat. Urgent looks were swapped across the table. For some inexplicable reason Esther wanted to cry.

Glancing up, Dunn saw them watching him and his mouth fell open.

"Shame to waste a good drop of soup," he smiled. "And this is a truly spondoolish slurp."

He always made up words when he spoke to the children. It was like a private joke between them, just as it had been between him and his wife when they were first married.

The children nodded their heads madly and looked down at their own meals. But Dunn was determined to pursue his conversation.

"I say nothing beats hot soup on these icy nights. Especially with the heating now as irregular as it is. Why, you're not eating, Miss Esther. You should. I've always thought you should eat more. And you, Master Carl, you don't wait till your food cools down properly. I've noticed the way that your eyes water."

Dunn flashed a grin at Frankie, who obligingly grinned back. He at least was happy. Having a new occupant in the master's seat was order to

23

his little world. As Dunn kept winking at him to refuel his grin, the two other boys glowered across at Esther, implying that, as Dunn's favourite, she should voice their feelings of outrage.

At last Esther spoke, her little voice hardly reaching the table's end.

"Will you clear away the soup things now, Mr Dunn. I don't think any of us are that hungry any more."

At this Dunn threw back his head and laughed goodnaturedly. "Why, Miss Esther, I haven't told you the cockahoo news yet. We got us a new serving-man."

With these words he rang the bell.

Presently, a sly-eyed youth, with terrible acne, opened the door. He was dressed in butler weeds, one of Dunn's old suits in fact, which seemed to swamp him and make him look ridiculously young.

"Yeah?"

"Yeah, *sir*!" corrected Dunn, bristling slightly. "Besides, I learnt you to say 'You rang, sir'. If you can't do this properly there's plenty others that'll – "

"You rang, s-ir," said the youth grandly, restoring the proprietary smile to Dunn's face.

"Ah, Blackhead, m'boy. You may serve the meat course now."

"Pronto, Mr Dunn, sir."

Under the table Carl kicked Esther. Her words shot out too quickly. "Mr Dunn," she said, "we think the weather is growing worse. You may go home now before the drifts get any deeper."

But Dunn only laughed again. "Why, you must be a mind reader, Miss Esther. Weren't I just coming to my second item of good news. My dear wife and I are moved into the big house. When she is more settled, she will accompany me at the dinner table. But the excitement of the move has brought on one of her nervy heads. Now don't that make you feel that much more secure? I can use my old musket on burglars instead of wolves, or the rats of course. Aren't you always complaining of the rats scrootling around and keeping you from your sleep, Miss Esther?"

With a defeated expression, Esther nodded once and pushed her hands into her lap.

Chapter Three

"Well, I think Dunn is a big fat stinky poo," Carl was saying. He was hunched up, his hands thrust deep into his pockets. When Blackhead slid past carrying crockery and flashing a smile as greasy as the top plate, they lowered their eyes. Still staring at the floor, Carl muttered: "What can we do?"

Zachary blinked his large owlish eyes behind his glasses. "It seems everybody's behaving as they shouldn't," he said. "Everybody but us."

"We shouldn't change," protested Carl. "We should be setting an example. We should be giving the orders. But pooey Dunn just has to smile and you know it's him that everyone listens to. I hate him and that spotty Blackhead too."

"That's not what I'm saying," continued Zachary. "What I mean is, well . . . *I* would like to do things that *I* have never done before."

"Such as?" asked Esther eagerly.

"For a start, I should like to go into rooms that were forbidden to us when the master was here. Explore a little."

Carl shrugged. "Too late now. It's almost bedtime. Tomorrow—"

"Why tomorrow? And who says we have to go to bed at 8.30 or 9.30 or whenever? Let's do what we want."

Carl was itching to follow Zachary but, shrugging his shoulders, feigned indifference.

"Well," said Esther, "I have often wondered – "

"What the master's private rooms are like!" shouted Zachary. "We all have. Let's go and look now. At last we can see for ourselves."

Esther, needing no further encouragement, grabbed Frankie's hand to make him run. He was yawning. By the time they reached the staircase sweeping up to the master's private rooms, she was practically dragging him. But Frankie wasn't only tired. He was afraid. The master had always frightened him. With big rounded eyes he stared up at the huge sign hanging over the foot of the stairs. On it, in massive letters, was the word:

SILENCE

Frankie couldn't read, but he understood. It meant no talking, no fun, long faces.

"Oh hurry up. Please, Frankie," urged Esther, in a voice both impatient and pleading.

Frankie hung his head and dragged his heels. At the top of the stairs was a door. A second sign upon it read:

ONLY THE PERMITTED NEED GO ANY FURTHER

It was unbearably tempting, yet before it they came to a halt.

"Shall we knock first?" whispered Carl.

Esther considered this. "Why should we? Who on earth could be there?" But she too was whispering.

Zachary settled matters by trying the handle. The warp of the ancient wood caused the door to spring open by an inch.

Carl swallowed. "You go first," he whispered to Zachary.

"No, you."

"I'm not going," said Esther.

And they whispered and called each other cowards until Carl said: "What about Frankie? Let's send Frankie first." More frantic whispering followed.

"What if it's booby-trapped?" argued Zachary.

"Like a crossbow tied to the handle?" suggested Esther. "Or even a bomb?"

"Huh," sneered Carl, pointing towards the SILENCE sign again. In any case, Frankie could not be induced to do anything which meant letting go of Esther's hand. Then Zachary settled matters by nudging the door with his foot. The force was greater than he intended, for the door slowly swung open.

"What can you see? What can you see?" cried Esther.

But all there was to see was darkness. It took a moment to realize that the darkness wasn't real. It was an effect created by everything in the room beyond the door being black, from the candles on the mantelpiece, to the faces of the clocks, to the walls and carpets and chandelier above. There was even a black painting in a black frame. Breaking the rule of black was a large fire and, beyond the dark window, the white snow. Falling snow swept the glass.

The children rushed upon the window first, examining a view that once only the master had enjoyed. They could hardly see the forest.

"There!" cried Carl pointing. "A wolf! A wolf! I saw a wolf! They must be getting hungry."

Of course it may have been a shadow. Snow and shadow were cast together, especially where the forest began. But now was the time for wolves. Sometimes they grew so hungry they fell upon each other. Dunn had his musket, so perhaps it wouldn't be so bad having him there after all. Zachary shuddered and drew away. When the others turned they saw him framed in a new doorway. He had opened the door and the glow of colour lured them to his side. Their gaze fell upon the master's bedchamber.

"Look!' cried Carl. "His bed is like a roundabout."

But there was so much to see. After the black room, it overwhelmed them.

The ceiling was a glorious make-believe sky with clouds, and birds, and swags of flowers, and a sun shooting out its rays like spears. The walls were not papered but clothed in evening suits of various colours and there were stuffed peacocks everywhere. The furniture looked ancient and heavy but much of it was obscured beneath yellowing photographs and cheap bric-à-brac. On the walls were no pictures, but over the dressing-table were embroidered texts from the Bible, each one beginning with "Thou shalt not".

Coming so far, the children were not going to deny their curiosity now. The drawers and cupboards soon yielded up their stiff shirt collars, hat boxes, watchchains and cufflinks. They became helpless with giggles at the master's whale-bone corsets and false moustaches, even more so when Zachary pulled on a corset and finished off the effect with a top hat. Esther found a long beaver-skin coat and curly wig and Carl slipped into a monogrammed dressing-gown and donned a hair-net. As for Frankie – they glanced around.

'Where's Frankie?" asked Zachary, slowly removing his hat.

"Frankie! Frankie!"

They found him in the roundabout-bed, sound asleep.

"Sloped off to bed, eh?" said Carl slyly.

"He's only pretending," said Esther.

They looked at each other and grinned. The next moment they had leapt under the blankets with him.

"Go 'way!" wailed Frankie.

They gripped the sheet and pulled it up to their noses. Then Carl reached out and tugged a cord. Immediately half the bed became enclosed with a heavy curtain. Esther, pulling a similar cord, caused the entire bed to be curtained off.

If, in the gloom, they smiled at their mischief, these smiles were soon wiped away by the sound of a door opening and a woman's shrill voice.

"Miss Pursglove! Miss Pursglove! Hurry up! Bring that tape-measure with you."

It was Aphid Dunn.

"Coming, madam. You go too fast for me. I declare myself quite breathless."

The second voice belonged to Aphid's new maid, Millicent Pursglove. A silly creature with a weakness for elbow-length gloves and ridiculously small hats.

"What a vulgar room," observed Dunn's wife with a sniff. "Too much blue, even for a sky, and will you look at this stuff strewn over the floor.

Looting. That's what it is. Some servants are no better than looters these days."

"It's truly criminal," agreed Miss Pursglove. "And with so many people in the world starving."

"What?"

Miss Pursglove tittered nervously. It was the laugh of a fieldmouse – if magnified a hundred times; and if able to laugh in the first place.

"Do you know, servants are stupid creatures."

"Oh, surely not. Not all," wailed Miss Pursglove, aware of her own situation.

"Brains of mules. Listen, I found twenty-three suits and sets of silken underwear laid out for the old master. One for each day since he upped and cleared off. When I questioned this, do you know what I was told? I was told that clean clothes were set out each morning. It was the rule and it wasn't a servant's place to go changing it. So I told them, before I dismissed the lot of them, what would the master do *if* he came back? Wear twenty-three sets of drawers beneath twenty-three pairs of trousers?"

Miss Pursglove tittered again.

"Hold this tape, Pursglove," ordered Aphid. "What does it say?"

"Oh, Mrs Dunn. I'm not wearing my proper spectacles. Oh. I require my reading ones and—"

"What are you doing peering through that

bottle, Pursglove?" Aphid's voice rose up in exasperation.

"M-magnifying, Mrs Dunn. I'm trying to make the numbers larger."

"Brains of mules!" stormed Aphid.

Inside the enclosed bed, the temperature was mounting. Uncomfortably hot in their clothes, the children could only lie still and listen as Aphid stomped around the room, measuring this, condemning that, and seeing faint possibilities for whatever remained.

"She's trying to take over the world," whispered Carl.

"Shhh," breathed Esther.

"It's true. You see."

Chapter Four

Aphid, in a turban and housecoat, showed herself the following morning. She announced herself with, "I have a headache," even as she was coming through the doors. Miss Pursglove followed six steps behind. Six of Aphid's steps, that is, which were equivalent to twelve of her own. This was why she looked hot and flustered. She carried Aphid's knitting-bag.

"Good morning, dearest," beamed Dunn, sitting at the head of the table, his bowler cocked upon the back of the master's chair.

Aphid did not reply. She patrolled the table, glaring at each child in turn. "I see we have visitors," she said.

This was too much for Carl. "You are the visitors!" he cried. "We always eat our breakfast here."

Aphid rooted her feet to the ground and her terrible glare upon Carl. "Miss Pursglove!" she summoned.

Flustered, like a chicken that senses a fox, Miss Pursglove ran to Aphid's side. She looked comical as she moved her head back and forth, trying to match the glare of her mistress when she looked towards Carl, then appearing obedient and servile when she turned to Aphid. Sometimes she failed to match the expression to the person.

"Take," spat Aphid, "take that child's name and give him one less potato at dinner. If he persists in his churlish behaviour he will gradually lose all his dinner. I will starve good manners into these wild things."

"Very g-good, Mrs D-Dunn." Aphid having now sat down, Miss Pursglove could no longer continue the same degree of ferocity towards Carl who, in any case, met her eye with a cold remorseless stare. She fumbled for her pocket book and pencil.

"For heaven's sake, Pursglove!" roared Aphid.

"Ah. Ah. Here they are. N-Now you must g-give me your n-name. At once. Or I'll see t-that you do—"

"My name is Carl," said Carl frostily.

Miss Pursglove, who couldn't spell Carl, wrote *Boy*.

Meantime Aphid had brought out her knitting

and finished two rows before Miss Pursglove finally drew up a footstool and sat beside her. The maid stretched out her arms as if pleading. Casually Aphid dropped a loop of wool over Miss Pursglove's wrists and began to wind a ball so rapidly that her bony hands became a blur. As she wound, she spoke. It was as if only Dunn was in the room with her.

"I had a terrible night's sleep, Mr Dunn. In our old house it were bad enough with the trees tapping the windows, but here it's worse. All night, right above my head, they were scratching away. Rats, Mr Dunn. Right above my poor face. And when I closed my eyes for a wink of rest, I imagined them rats dropping on to me and doing me damage. I've heard stories of rats carrying off babies, Mr Dunn. No wonder I'm full of the frets this morning.'

She stopped winding with an abruptness that made Miss Pursglove jump. Incredulously she stared at Dunn who had risen and crossed to Frankie. With his handkerchief he was wiping Frankie's face which was sticky with scrambled egg and butter. Afterwards he offered him a clean corner and said gently: "A nice big nozzleblast for Mr Dunn," and Frankie blew his nose.

"Well, if that doesn't beat everything," said Aphid in a nasty dry voice. "That takes the biscuit. I'm discussing discomfort and possible danger to my person while my husband sees that wet noses are blown clean."

"I was still listening to every word, dearest," said Dunn, in an appeasing tone.

"That is not the point," retorted Aphid, leaning forward and tapping out her words with a knitting needle. "What I want to know is, why that child is allowed to sit at the same table as mannered folk in the first place. It quite turns my stomach the way he eats, with his mouth gaping so I can see every morsel he chews."

Frankie began to snivel. He sensed that he had become the centre of attention, which always made him feel uncomfortable. Raised voices cowered him.

"Frankie eats with us every day!" yelled Zachary. "And if we like it, you'll have to learn to like it too!"

Aphid blew out her cheeks as if affronted by the biggest insult known to man. Pointing at Zachary, she ordered Miss Pursglove to take his name and amend his rations accordingly. Poor Miss Pursglove. If she couldn't spell Carl she hadn't the faintest notion of how to write Zachary's name. With a shaking hand she wrote *Boy (2)*.

At that moment the doors opened and Blackhead stepped in carrying a steaming two-handled mug.

"Excuse me, madam," he said, giving Aphid

a faint nod. "I have taken a liberty . . . I 'eard you had a troubled 'ead."

Aphid looked at him like a startled bird. She recovered herself and took the mug. Dunn smiled his thanks at the youth and winked at the children, indicating that soon everything would be all right.

Chapter Five

The heating had broken down, yet again. To keep warm, the children decided to attend their dancing class. Herr Gaulard, the dancing master, looked up with indifference as they stood before him. He was a crooked raw-boned thing in two coats and a balaclava. Esther imagined that once his eyes had been brilliant blue, but now they were washed-out and bloodshot; and the skin about his jowls hung flabbily, with white whiskers lining the furrows.

He coughed as he rose, his breath white in the great ballroom. Slowly he crossed to a wind-up gramophone as ugly as an old-fashioned sideboard. As soon as he wound it up the crackles and spits began. Opening a door at either end of the machine he revealed the speakers; the wider doors were opened, the louder the music.

Coughing, Herr Gaulard returned to his stool and with a grunt reached down for his cane.

"De valtz," he announced. And, tapping out the beat, monotonously intoned: "Vun, Toh, Tree. Vun, Toh, Tree . . ."

Esther danced with Zachary. Frankie partnered Carl.

Minutes later: "De tango. Vun, Toh, Tree. Vun, Toh, Tree . . ."

Then: "De military toh step."

Sometimes Herr Gaulard's chesty cough got the better of him. He could continue to bang the floor until able to recommence with those three dull numbers.

"Vun, Toh, Tree . . ."

At other times the gramophone would slowly wind down, as would the dancers, until the dance-master struggled across to crank both back to their proper speeds.

Esther danced with elegance. Even dressed in a coat and scarf her movements seemed to make sense. Like an actress, she used her face to convey the soul of the dance. She did it deliberately. Softly sentimental and tilted to one side for the waltz. Proud and firm for the tango. Zachary loved these expressions. He had always been a little in awe of her. He danced well just to please her, but he was merely adequate compared with Esther.

"De fochstrot," announced Herr Gaulard,

gagging on a cough. "Vun, Toh, Tree. Vun, Toh, Tree . . ."

No matter what he called, Frankie and Carl always continued as before. Frankie was too excitable, so Carl's foot movements were dictated by a desire not to have them trampled upon.

Occasionally, as they danced, one of the titanic cast-iron radiators let out a chug or metallic clank, whereupon the dancers would stop and gaze hopefully at it. Yet each time the noise would fade and die, and each time the four children dutifully took up their partners and danced on.

"Vun, Toh, Tree. Vun, Toh, Tree . . ."

When the door swung open and Blackhead appeared with a tray of steaming cocoa mugs, the dancers simply fell apart and stared at him.

Irritably, Herr Gaulard scuttled to the gramophone to stop the record.

"*Ja?*"

"Excuse my intrusion and all that," smiled the youth confidently. "But as you ain't got no decent heating, I thought you may benefit from a bit of warming."

The four children fell upon the tray, but the old dancemaster waved away the mug Blackhead offered him.

"No? Then I'll not see it go to waste," smiled the youth, taking up the mug himself and sliding the tray under his elbow. "Ahh. Good stuff is what I say, and I says this too: we should all be shaking in our shoes what with so many 'ungry wolves in our midst."

"What do you mean?" asked Carl, lifting his head to face Blackhead with a cocoa moustache.

Blackhead looked around, making sure he had everyone's attention. Herr Gaulard, putting a record in its sleeve, refused to acknowledge him.

"It's like this, see," said Blackhead mysteriously. "The big blue parlour looks like something from the North Pole. The snow and ice has burst in through its frenchie windows and it's like Jack Frost's living-room in there now."

"Can wolves come in?" asked Carl, sparking with enthusiasm.

"In or out. They can come or go as easy as they please. If it weren't for a pretty stout door at the other end, why they could be roaming the house by now." He winked. "Imagine that, Miss Esther."

Esther shivered. "I'd rather not, thank you."

Zachary said: "The wind must have really got up – I mean, to blow open the doors like that."

Blackhead laughed. "That's just it, Master Zac," he said. (Zachary hated this chummy name.) "The doors were left open purposefully like. I suspects one of the servants Mr Dunn gave the boot to. Done it out of spite. Terrible thing though."

He tipped back his head and drained the last of his cocoa.

"Now, duty calls. If you wants for anything else, just shout for Blackhead. He's the one you want. Just shout. I ain't never far away."

He laughed and left them. Herr Gaulard drew attention to himself with a cough. He took out a yellow handkerchief, wiped his nose and returned it to his sleeve.

"Why don't we go and take a look at the parlour?" cried Zachary. "I'm sure you wouldn't mind, would you, Herr Gaulard?"

The dancing-master met Zachary's ingratiating smile with a frosty stare.

"You vant go see snow and ice, go see snow and ice," he said, breaking off with a cough.

Carl said mischievously: "You don't like Blackhead, do you?"

The vehemence of Herr Gaulard's reply took the smile off Carl's face. "Noh! Noh, I do not like him! Why he come here pretending to be nice? Big man. Big man. You stay vell away frrom him. He ist a big boy. He ist dangerous. You vant see snow and ice. Go. Go see it."

He shuffled on his stool and coughed. He did not reply when they called goodbye to him. Soon they were running down the corridor.

"And where are you off to, my pretties, at such a gallopalash?"

Dunn met them at the top of the stairs.

Around his head and bowler was a knotted scarf. Leaning against the bannister, he regarded the children with good-natured tolerance.

"To the blue parlour, Mr Dunn," replied Carl breathlessly. Both Zachary and Esther glowered at him. Dunn may forbid them now, using the wolves as an excuse to keep them away. But no. Dunn carefully did up the top button on Frankie's coat saying: "You do what you please, my pretties. Go and have fun. Enjoy yourselves. I likes seeing youngsters enjoy themselves as youngsters should."

He straightened Frankie's hat and sent them on their way.

Hardly had they rounded two more corners when they came upon a curious sight. It was Miss Pursglove. Her hair was tied up in knotted rags to make it wavy, and plastered upon her face was a face-pack as green as avocados. It emphasized her eyes and thin lips. A small piercing scream arose from those lips when the children almost collided with her. In contempt they stood watching, for suddenly she was animated like a wounded bird. Desperately she tried various doors, only to find them locked. She seemed all hands and feet. Her head darted and nodded.

"W-what do y-you children want h-here? Oh dear. Oh dear. Y-you better not hurt me. I'm st-stronger than I l-look you know. Why are these

44

l-locked? I w-want to p-pass. You must l-let me pass . . ."

Gradually her fluster was turning to a petulant anger. She verged on the hysterical.

"Oh dear. Oh dear."

A door abruptly opened. Aphid loomed large in a quilted dressing-gown and slippers. Seeing the hot-water bottles strapped to her body, Carl and Zachary sniggered. Luckily for them, Aphid failed to notice.

"What is the meaning of this hullabaloo? Pursglove, you ridiculous woman, take a grip on yourself. Explain yourself, lady. Here am I trying to rest me eyes after a night of being kept awake by vermin, and you won't even allow me that."

"Did the rats keep you awake?" asked Esther. "We have got used to them."

"Have you now?" rounded Aphid angrily. "Have you indeed? Then you are most fortunate children. Aren't you?"

Together they murmured: "Yes, Mrs Dunn."

They saw an interest in them suddenly come alive in her sharp face. She demanded to know where they were going. When told – they were too frightened to lie to her – she hugged a hot-water bottle to her bosom.

"Good," she said. "Play there. Play there all day. It's on the other side of the house. They won't disturb us there, will they, Miss Pursglove?"

45

"No, no. To be sure. No, Mrs Dunn."

The door closed, as Aphid withdrew into her room. Like a confused goose Miss Pursglove flapped off in the same instant.

"C'mon," said Carl, and turning towards Aphid's door he screwed up his face. "Poo-bag," he said. "I hope the rats climb into your bed. I hope they bite you when you're snoring your ugly head off."

To reach the blue parlour they slid down a heavy, carved bannister rail, all except Frankie who was afraid. "You wait me! You wait me!" he whinged as he clumsily clattered down the stairs. He could be tiresomely clingy when he was being a scaredy-cat.

The door to the parlour was of heavy panelled oak. Throwing it open they plunged into winter.

"Wow!"

"Ya-hoo!"

"Weeeee!"

Then suddenly they fell silent, hugging themselves with cold and awe.

The French window was fully open and now smooth banks of snow made it quite impossible to close. In a white shimmering slope, the snow reached into the room. At its powdery limit the rugs glowed through like embers. The children could hardly believe it. Icicles hung from the ceiling and door-heads. Drifts were caught in the laps of chairs and sofas. Snow bearded portraits, and frost rimmed the ornaments. Like dust it lay on the tables, thick enough for Carl to write his name. And all the time, sweeping through the open doorway, came a bitterly cold wind. It swirled angrily around the four walls and blew out again, flicking up the snow in its wake, as if with a tail.

The children spoke in respectful whispers, nudging each other to look at this or notice that. Then, holding each others' hands for balance, they waded as far as the French window to peer out. Snow nearly reached their waists. Ahead stretched the dark band of the forest, and where the lawns had been, sharp breezes whipped up snow flurries, while the ornamental bushes stood crushed and remoulded into shapeless white heaps.

Esther said: "I don't like it here. Let's go back."

"C-c-c-cold," shivered Frankie.

Carefully they struggled back through the deep drift and Zachary shook the oak door by its handle.

"What's wrong?" asked Carl.

"It's been locked."

Chapter Six

"It's no use," said Zachary, with a sob in his voice. "Nobody'll hear us. Nobody!"

They had hammered the heavy door and shouted until their fists and throats hurt. Esther perched herself demurely on a snowy chair. Carl cried, so Frankie did. The three of them turned to Zachary. He felt their eyes upon him. It's unfair to expect me to know all the answers, he thought bitterly. He got into the nervous routine of pushing his glasses up his nose. Cold numbed them as much as the idea that somebody had deliberately locked them in.

Suddenly Esther sprang to her feet. "It's no use sitting here," she said matter-of-factly. "We'll freeze. Carl, Frankie, stop crying at once. We'll be all right. We'll just have to go out and around the house until we find another door or window."

Her confidence carried the little band as far as the French window. Here a sudden sharp wind took the edge off it. The snow lay deep. And to their dismay they remembered that, on the left, stood the chapel with its high gothic windows and, on the right, the former powder-room, which barely boasted an opening at all. Already the light was beginning to dim. Darkness was quickly setting in. Candles would be lit and, throughout the house, stout shutters closed against the bitter cold.

"He-lp!" cried Esther, tilting back her head to throw her voice up the grey rise of balconies, windows and snowy ledges. Carl, Zachary, and even Frankie, instantly joined in her cry. But at that moment, the wind got up. It rushed down from the dreary forest and whipped across the gardens, bursting in a white spray around urns and cherubs and frozen fountains. Snow blew into their faces, until they could hardly hear each other.

Zachary's voice suddenly acquired a new urgency. "Quiet! All of you! Look!"

He pointed.

Despite the wind, something had indeed heard – not the shouts of terrified children, but the anxious bleats of food. Their blood ran cold. It was a wolf. Starved and ragged, it stood black and still, the snow almost reaching its middle.

Scrambling back into the parlour and out of the wind, they attacked the heavy door again; glancing back, as if through smoke, to see not one wolf, but four, each observing its prey with mild curiosity.

"He-lp! Please! You must help!"

The snow was turning grey as night rapidly descended. What colour remained in the parlour dimmed. The forest was a black spiky wall. Then, from within it, rose the first mournful howls of the pack, while in the garden their numbers had grown to seven, and they had crept nearer. Suddenly, from the trees, sprang a large long-haired she-wolf. She came ploughing through the snow, growling; her intentions obvious enough to rouse the others. All at once, a baying pack of wolves was careering through the drifts, in an arc that grew ever more well-defined as it closed in on that snowy room.

The children were no longer shouting for help, but screaming with terror.

A voice spoke.

"Here. Come on. Hurry up!"

It came from behind, drawing them like a magnet, causing them to stumble over chairs and each other like panicked blind-men. The voice belonged to a girl and came from an opening that had simply appeared in the wall. Piling in, the opening closed behind them; and now they crouched in a passageway, hearing the wolves' frustrated snarls echoing as if from a long way away.

For a few minutes they could do nothing more than weep and cling to each other.

By her lantern, the girl who had saved them watched, partly puzzled and partly amused. She was a short dumpy girl, rather plain, with basin-cropped hair, a round face and mocking eyes. She was dressed in mended clothes and carried a stick, set into which was a kitchen knife.

"Have you finished blubbing yet?" she asked. "If I'd known you were such roarers I'd've rescued you sooner."

Esther brushed away her tears with the back of a wrist. "You mean you were spying on us when you could have rescued us all the time?"

The girl detected a note of criticism. "Could have left you," she replied defensively. "Nobody asked you to go into that room. Besides, what've you ever done for me?"

They fell quiet. Then a squabble broke out over whose turn it was to wipe Frankie's nose. Esther caught the girl's eye.

"My name is—"

"I know who you are. All of you. I know well enough to realize I'll not be thanked by anyone at the house for rescuing you, let alone rewarded."

They waited for her to introduce herself, but it needed Carl to ask.

The girl said: "If you must know, my name is Oonagh."

"Where do you live?" asked Zachary tentatively.

The girl – Oonagh – threw back her head and laughed so loudly that it echoed along the passage. The wolves heard it and once more began to snarl.

"Live? I live here, you numbskull. I'm one of the Rats. We live in the pipes and the underground places of your grand house.'

The four children had plenty to occupy their thoughts as Oonagh led them along a twisting passageway.

Somebody had deliberately tried to kill them by pushing the bolt across the parlour door. But who? Blackhead had whetted their interest in the room. And Dunn, his wife, and even Miss Pursglove knew they were going there. One had shot the bolt across, and why one? What about any combination of the four working together? Great care must be taken from now on. These were dangerous times.

And, just as extraordinary, was this Oonagh girl. One of the Rats, she said; so how many like her were hidden away in the pipes and sewers and beneath the floors? An entire tribe! Zachary in particular itched to ask more, but Oonagh had shut herself off from answering further questions and they made their way in silence.

At last she turned, saying fiercely: "You must

go through this door now. Never try to open it again. Never! Understand? Really I should have left you for the wolves. If you want to thank me for saving you, just forget about me, the sooner the better."

They nodded, but began to thank her all the same. Oonagh threw open a low rectangular door and roughly pushed them through. When it was closed again, the four children saw that it was the blackboard in their schoolroom. On it was scrawled: *Gorgio you angle. I love you with every fibre of my being. A million kisses. Eternal love. Amelia Frost.*

"Yuk!" scowled Carl.

Zachary pointed at the word *angle*. "She means angel," he said, pushing his glasses up his nose. "She was never very good at spelling."

Chapter Seven

Esther told herself to observe their faces: Dunn, Mrs Dunn, Blackhead and Miss Pursglove. The expressions of the guilty would surely give their game away.

At dinner time they came together to eat.

A fire was leaping up the chimney and candles flickered, distorting on the silverware, and brightly lighting every face. Esther peered hard. Miss Pursglove was as flustered as usual. "My fan, my fan. Dear. I seem to have mislaid it." Fan! It was chilly enough in that room without radiators, and she wittered for fans. Wearing his most ingratiating smile, Blackhead nodded and bowed to anyone who caught his eye; and Mrs Dunn was preoccupied with her *boys*, one of whom had been *naughty* on the carpet. Of course Blackhead obliged by cleaning up the mess, even patting the head of the offending animal. Mrs Dunn smiled a brief tight-lipped smile at him. It reminded Esther of poison.

As for Dunn, he barely noticed the children at all. His thoughts were elsewhere. Freely he helped himself to the claret, and he sat slumped in his chair. On meeting Esther's eye, he turned away as if ashamed.

Dunn! It must be Dunn! Esther began to ache and grow hot with anger and, more curiously, pity.

Just then Dunn reached for his drink and knocked it over. The red wine soaked into the tablecloth, spreading like blood. Aphid tutted. Blackhead rushed to mop up the spill, but Dunn waved him away. "Leave it be, damn you!" he roared, his voice hoarse with drink. "Let things be at this end of the table at least."

Then the children noticed that one chair was missing. Aphid extended her poisonous smile to them.

"It's that child there." She gestured at Frankie. (Couldn't she bring herself to use his name?) "I think it rather unseemly having an *invalid* mangling and spilling his food at my table, so I have made other arrangements."

"Frankie?" uttered Zachary. "The master always liked him to sit beside him at meal times. He even cut up his food for him."

"Master this, master that," snarled Aphid.

"He didn't know everything you know."

"But what are you going to do with him?" demanded Carl.

"Do?" Aphid smiled again. "Do? I'm not going to make a pie of him, boy, if that's what you mean. He must go and eat behind that screen. I assure you it'll be better for him too. If I were him I'd be distressed watching folk use knives and forks in a proper manner and not be able to do so m'self."

"Rest assured," oozed Blackhead. "I'll take the very best care of the little fella."

Reluctantly the children seated themselves. Frankie was led away behind a Chinese lacquered screen. "Who's a good lickle boy then? Who's going to be a good lickle chap and eat up all his din-dins?" they could hear Blackhead drone. Dunn poured himself another drink and, catching Esther's eye a second time, faced her squarely and apologetically.

Perhaps it wasn't Dunn, she thought. Perhaps he was feeling guilty about Frankie.

Unsteadily Dunn got to his feet to carve the joint.

"Let's get this damn beef hacked," he said.

Miss Pursglove twisted her swan-like neck and addressed her mistress. "My dear Mrs Dunn, may I say how much more refreshed you look. Did you sleep well?"

"Sleep!" spat Aphid. "I would pay good

money for a decent night's sleep. A whole lot of money. But I sleep so light. The slightest scritch or scratch has me awake again. I will not have a moment's rest while this house is allowed to teem with vermin.' She clasped her arms about her and nervously stroked her elbows.

The children exchanged glances. Dunn said in a dull voice: "All big homes has their rats. It's only as it has been."

Aphid snorted, making her face even more unpleasant. "Don't have to have them. No need to encourage them."

Miss Pursglove twittered as if at something amusing. "Whatever do you mean, my dear Mrs Dunn?"

Aphid straightened herself in her chair and fixed her eyes on Dunn. "Why, my dear Miss Pursglove. It's absurd. Today I discover that food has been left out for those disgusting vermin. Not just a few crumbs either but practically half a larder. And a servant existed under this very roof just for the purpose of feeding them. It was the master's way, he claimed. Master's way or not, it's not the way of common sense, says I; and I dismissed the servant at once and had all the food taken back to the kitchens."

Esther noticed that Dunn was cutting the meat erratically as if angry. She could also make out Blackhead's voice from behind the screen, this time dark and menacing. "Eat up your cabbage, ninny," came the cruel whisper, "or the wolves'll get you. D'ya hear, blockhead?"

Esther found herself torn between the two conversations.

With a clatter Dunn dropped the carving implements. Everyone looked up, startled. Dunn's expression towards his wife melted, turning pathetically hound-doggish. "There has always been rats in this house, dearest," he repeated softly.

"I don't deny it," snapped Aphid. "All I say is, I can't see why they should go on being encouraged. Surely the well-being of your wife is worth that, Mr Dunn?"

Miss Pursglove giggled. She had taken two small sips of her wine and was hopelessly tiddly. 'Perhaps we should call in the rat-catcher."

"An excellent suggestion, my dear Miss Pursglove," agreed Aphid. "As I see it, the man we need is Moses Mummery."

At the name, Miss Pursglove gave a small scream.

"For goodness' sake, lady," said Aphid irritably, "don't keep going on so alarmingly. He may not be the pleasantest of men, but at least he'll be thorough in what he does. Those rumours about h—"

At that moment, Frankie gave a shout of rage. He must have kicked out with his foot too, for the Chinese screen folded, and crashed down around him. Turning, they saw Blackhead straddling Frankie in an armchair, pinning him down and forcing a spoon into his mouth.

"HATE CABBAGE!" yelled Frankie, throwing it aside.

Carl leapt up and now his voice joined the commotion. "You leave him be! You hear! You let him alone!"

"Sit down, child," said Aphid crisply. "This is a table to eat at, not a public meeting-place."

Rounding on her in his anger, Carl shouted: "You shut up too, you ... you ... big poo bum!"

The room went quiet save for Frankie's soft whimpering. Miss Pursglove looked to Aphid, awaiting her cue to be suitably mortified. As for Aphid, she clutched her chest as if from a physical blow. When her words came she was unable to finish a sentence.

"Why ... Never in all my days ... When I was a girl, children were ... It's scandalous ..."

"That child deserves a beating," said Miss Pursglove, who then blushed at her forwardness.

"He needs manners learning him," agreed Aphid breathlessly. "Miss Pursglove, write down this creature's name at once. Write: no dinner for a week, no meat, no sugar for his tea. Well, Mr Dunn. What do *you* intend to do about this dreadful display of inadequate upbringing? These children have been left to roam wild for too long. They are a tribe of untameable little savages."

Dolefully Dunn rose to his feet. "Come, Master Carl," he said.

With head hung, Carl followed him into an adjoining chamber. He watched Dunn lift a cushion and remove a strut from a chair. When Dunn stood, Carl began to undo his trousers, but Dunn smiled a marvellous, mischievous smile. He held a finger before his lips, saying gravely: "You must be taught to respect your elders, Master Carl. Be brave and take your punishment manfully."

Thereupon he brought the strut down with a resounding whack on the back of a sofa. He pointed at Carl. "Ow!" squawked Carl obligingly.

Whack!

"Ahh!"

Whack!

"Oh please, Mr Dunn!"

Whack!

"Ooh!"

Dunn put a hand across his mouth to scupper the giggles. Handing the strut to Carl he watched him amble around the room, taking swipes at the furniture and afterwards crying out as if in pain.

Soon the room was fuzzy with dust.

Beckoning Carl to him, Dunn wetted his

finger and carefully painted tears on to the boy's face.

"There, Master Carl," he said severely. "Let that be a lesson to you."

Chapter Eight

The name of Moses Mummery was whispered throughout the house and never before had the rats had so many allies. Leah, the French maid, claimed she would leave the house if *that man* ever set foot in it. Mr Hunter-Spruce, the underwine superintendent, stated he would not stoop to serve him, while Mr Doyle from the boiler room told everyone that, if there was an ounce of justice in this world, Moses Mummery would have been strung up years ago.

It was the sole topic of conversation.

Moses Mummery, it was wildly held, was a vampire. Twenty years ago a series of brutal child murders had taken place. Nothing was proven, but Mummery had been hounded from his village into the stark friendless depths of the forest, away from his fellow men.

"But who's going to send word to him?" asked Carl. "Everywhere is heaped over in snow and wolves."

"Blackhead," said Esther gloomily.

Zachary nodded. "He would jump through a hoop to please Dunn and his wife."

They were in their schoolroom. The heating had again broken down. It was gloomy, with light the colour of tin coming through the iced window. Although each of them wore three jumpers, they were still cold. Zachary crouched to poke the grate where some books glowed but refused to burn. They had chosen their least favourite books to burn first: *Elementary Physics*, *Precise Language Use* and *McGonagall's Rules of Mathematics*. Esther held Miss Frost's diary in her lap, refusing to burn it. Occasionally, she tried to read a passage, although there were many words she didn't understand, and they had burnt Dr Johnson's Dictionary yesterday, toasting bread by the life's work of the grand old lexicographer.

A little apart from the others, hugging his knees, sat Carl. He listened carefully to all that was said. It was perhaps then he decided. He would keep watch on Blackhead and when Blackhead went to fetch Moses, he would somehow warn the Rats. A Rat had saved their lives. They couldn't sit back now while the Rats were exterminated.

Carl began visiting the stables. He made himself a den covered in hay. It was súrprisingly warm amongst the horses, and the stable lads humoured the small boy by giving him chocolate biscuits and old horse-shoes. Sometimes Carl took Frankie with him and Frankie, once warm, would fall asleep in one of the empty stalls. Otherwise Carl kept his watch a secret from the others. He relished the secrecy.

Then, four days later, he heard a sharp, shrill voice. He pulled a face and lay low. It was Aphid, dismissing the stable-hands, telling them to go and wait in the snow. Through the straw he watched her, swathed in white fur, slink into the stables. She had that thin poisonous smile upon her face. Blackhead, walking a few paces behind, occasionally cocked his head to shoot her a quizzical sideways glance. He was wearing one of the master's coats. It was slightly too large for him, making him appear boyish.

"Pick any horse you want, Blackhead," said Aphid with a brittle brightness. "Take your time. Choose with care. Time taken in picking a good animal now is not time wasted."

Blackhead nodded. He shifted from foot to foot. Clearly her over-friendliness was embarrassing to him.

"You still believe you can carve out your way alone?" she asked abruptly, still fixing him with her smile.

"Don't need no one," mumbled Blackhead darkly. "Ain't done so badly so far."

"Listen, you idiot. How many more times do I have to say it? I need you to help me. Everything is up for grabs – surely you see that? Just as you can see that Dunn's not the man to do it. It's been me so far, Aphid Dunn, who's made all the running and taken the risks. I'm ambitious you see, Blackhead. I'm not one who's ashamed to admit it. I like the best things I can have from life. But I need someone like you to help me get them. Besides, there is more than enough for both of us here."

"You misunderstand me, Mrs Dunn. I'm just your old man's second-in-command. I try to do a good job."

"Don't give me that," said Aphid, with a knowing smile. "I've been watching you. Watching you closely."

For the first time Blackhead looked up with fierceness. "I don't steal, I don't cook the books and I ain't no cheat," he said. "I keep me nose clean."

"Precisely," returned Aphid. "Which probably makes you unique in this house. It makes me think that if you'll not chance your neck on the crumbs you're probably saving it for something bigger?" She smiled again.

Blackhead turned away. He gestured at the horses. "Had a word with the bloke beforehand," he said, talking fast. "Told me all this horsemeat is much of a muchness. Ain't no difference in any of 'em. Take that 'un. White – like the snow." He laughed humourlessly.

Aphid watched silently as the youth saddled his chosen horse. When he swung himself into the saddle, Carl saw the long sword at his side.

"Think about it, Blackhead," said Aphid. "And you will take care."

"Ain't the wolves that scare me," replied Blackhead in a low voice. "Understand them. It's their nature to be fierce. You want me to fetch Old Man Mummery, Mrs Dunn. I'll do me best. Can't promise anything mind. Might not want to travel through this weather."

"You must persuade him," said Aphid, stroking the white mare on which Blackhead sat bolt upright. "Old men have few desires, but the promise of a warm bed and good food should bring him. Old men are basically greedy. It's *their* nature. Like the wolves."

Taking the bridle, Aphid slowly led the horse out of the building, into the crushed yellow snow of the courtyard beyond.

When the stable was again full of its usual workers and friendly voices, Carl bolted from his hiding place. Straw was still in his hair when he found the other three.

"He's gone!"

"Who?"

"Blackhead, of course. He's gone to fetch Moses. Mrs Dunn has sent him. And Moses will murder all the Rats. We've got to warn them."

The others looked at him, dumbfounded. But Carl had already thought things through. Without a pause for breath his words came tumbling out.

"We could try to break into the Rats' tunnel by chopping through the blackboard," he said. "But Oonagh warned us not to do that, and she'll probably get into big trouble with the other Rats. Besides, we'll only end up lost. So I have a better idea. If the Rats live in the drains, perhaps we could shout down to them and warn them that way."

"But all the drains are outside," said Esther, "and covered in snow."

Carl regarded her angrily for not understanding his plan. "Don't be so stupid, Esther. Not all the drains are outside. What about those in the bathrooms?"

Esther turned to Zachary. He shrugged. "It's worth a try," he said.

They raced to the nearest bathroom as if there wasn't a moment to lose. It was cold and bare and smelt of pine disinfectant. The grandiose porcelain gleamed and was decorated with bright blue patterns. Shells, dolphins and mermaids. As Zachary kept watch, Esther and Carl scrambled from bath to sink, shouting their warnings. Zachary, however, could hardly make out a word above Frankie's helpless laughter.

Chapter Nine

It was night in the big house. Esther lay in her bed that was so large it was permanently cold about its edges and corners. As tired as she was, she could not sleep. Her thoughts were like a dimly-lit theatre. On its stage she saw Blackhead riding his white mare, the horse stumbling through drifts of snow, wolves surrounding them. In her mind Esther urged the creatures to drag Blackhead down but spare the horse. But her thoughts would not be controlled. The scene changed. Now there were two riding the horse: Blackhead was returning through the midnight-black forest with Moses Mummery. Better the wolves get both, thought Esther. But the figure of Mummery was like dense smoke. The wolves, more afraid than hungry, drew back and back—

"I said, 'You asleep?' And you said, 'No'. But

you were." The voice was sneering but amused.

"Who is it?" demanded Esther sleepily.

"Only a friendly Rat," said the voice.

Something heavy landed on the end of the bed. Esther rocked. She felt indignant, but more than that, she felt oddly happy too.

"The girl!" she cried. "You're that girl, Oonagh. It's Oonagh, isn't it? The girl who saved us from the wolves."

"What if I am?"

Esther didn't reply. She sensed Oonagh looking about the room.

"Cold here," sniffed the girl. "Shame we make you suffer with Dunn and his crew. But when you sabotage the heating you can't go making special allowances for no one."

Esther understood only slowly. "You've made our heating break down? Why?"

"You don't feed us Rats. We don't take care of the pipes. That's the deal. Or rather, not the deal. The master understood. He left food out for us. Payment. But la-di-da Lady Dunn has stopped all that, so us Rats don't do our bit either."

"You know she's sent Blackhead to fetch Moses Mummery. He's coming to exterma-, extermana-, to *murder* all you Rats."

This amused Oonagh vastly. She threw back her head and hooted with laughter, in a way

70

which Esther had learnt was quite unladylike at her poise and manners classes.

"'Course we knew about Moses Mummery. We knew long before you went broadcasting it around the plumbing. There's no need to shout, y'know. Rats have pretty good hearing."

"Sorry."

"No. It was good of you." Oonagh's voice had softened. "The Rats now know their friends. Don't worry. We won't let Mummery hurt you."

"But . . ." Esther was confused.

Oonagh sighed as if spelling out the obvious. "Listen. The Rats are a nuisance, but you – the kids of the house – you are a threat. More than one person under this roof has big plans. You, just by living and breathing, spoil them. The master's will hasn't been found yet and you may be named as sole inheritors."

Esther said: "Mind if I light my lamp? I want to see you."

"Go ahead, light it. You'll need it in the pipes."

"Pipes?"

"Don't deny it. You'd love to look beneath the house at the Rats' run. It took a lot of argy-bargy but I did it. I persuaded the other Rats to let you come. Are you dressed?"

"'Course I am. I'm wearing three cardies and two pairs of socks. You turned the heating off, remember?"

"So we did," said Oonagh, and throwing back

71

her head, honked with laughter like a goose.

Although she had entered the room from above, dropping down on to Esther's bed, Oonagh now led the way to the window, whose crisp moonlit shape glowed faintly through the curtains. Esther held up the lamp as Oonagh swept the cushions from a window-seat and lifted the wooden base.

"I don't need no light," said Oonagh. "You save it for yourself."

Esther turned down the lamp and guided herself into a sloping passage, whose mouth was the window-seat base.

"Close the hatch behind you," ordered Oonagh.

Carefully Esther lowered the seat and began stepping down a tight flight of little steps.

"Come on," mocked Oonagh's voice somewhere near the bottom.

"It's all right for you!" cried Esther without thinking. "You're a Rat!"

The raucous laughter of the wild girl came floating up the stairs.

Esther didn't really know what to expect. Perhaps a dreary hole, cramped and wet and smelly. But it wasn't a bit like that. At the bottom of the steps was an airy tunnel, which Esther was a good way along before realizing it wasn't a tunnel at all, but a pipe. It arched overhead in the light of her lamp and its sides slid smoothly round and under her feet. Not that it impaired her ability to walk. Her steps made a faint metallic ring as she followed Oonagh.

Then Oonagh stopped. She wanted to show Esther something. She was pointing at the side. But try as she might Esther could not understand what it was.

"The welding," explained Oonagh, exasperated. "See, still as good as the day it was made. And as smooth." She ran her fingers along it, stroking it as she would a cat.

Further along the pipe narrowed. Other pipes joined it, and little brass pipes criss-crossed overhead. Oonagh thought Esther's education incomplete, so she wasn't content to let any of these things pass by. She pointed out universal joints, lead collars, and double S-bends; while Clackson's noble flush-trap obviously filled her with admiration.

"Beautiful," she murmured to herself.

The larger pipes formed their own complete highways yet they met no one else. Esther was half-glad about this. The underworld of the house had a forbidding air about it. She felt she was trespassing. Still, it would have been interesting, meeting other Rat people. It was like something she had once read about rain-forests. Long lost tribes that weren't really lost at all, but there all the time, hidden amongst the arching ferns and thickly spreading trees. Presently she heard water.

"Save your lamp for going back," said Oonagh, blowing it out for her. In the steely-grey half-light Esther saw Oonagh grinning.

"Come on," she said.

As they went forward, the sound of water grew stronger along with the light, which had a liquid, shimmering quality. The pipe stopped abruptly and Esther stood on the brink of a large underground lake.

"What's this?" she asked.

"The reservoir," Oonagh replied, adding: "Your future bath water."

"And those bright lights over there?"

"My home. The house-boat. Where I live with Man O'Dea."

Climbing down some steps and entering a small rowing boat, Oonagh explained that Man O'Dea had found her floating in a basket, and adopted her because he didn't know who her real parents were.

"Had he not come along at that moment," Oonagh added casually, "I would have sunk without a trace. The basket had already sprung a leak and, as it was, I was pretty sick for weeks after. So Man tells me anyway."

Esther nodded. "So he's like a father," she said, for she liked to have everything neatly ordered in her thoughts.

Oonagh doubled up with laughter. The boat shook with her gulps. "You are peculiar," she said.

Pulling her lips tightly together, Esther resolved to be silent and then to make some sneering remark at the next thing Oonagh said, no matter how mundane. But then she heard something extraordinary that made her cry out.

"Sit still!" ordered Oonagh harshly. "You'll have us both in the water."

"But didn't you hear?"

"It's only The Whispers," said Oonagh, paddling on.

Across the water, hissing like a ghostly wind, came a voice. It was Aphid's. Now and then Esther could catch her words.

"How . . . sleep . . . Dunn? . . . rats . . . nerves snapping . . . But soon . . . But soon . . ."

Then, criss-crossing Aphid's voice, came another. A servant was talking to his dog. Soon, yet a third came gusting over the lake: a maid's complaint at having to undress in the cold. Three separate conversations in different quarters of the house. Overlapping, rising and falling. Oonagh, indifferent, pushed the paddle in and pulled it out. Esther gripped the boat's sides. The reservoir was a natural receptacle for every noise in the house. No wonder the Rats knew about the arrival of Moses Mummery.

The rowing boat bumped the side of the

house-boat. It was a long unpainted vessel with a single mast and a washing-line filled with washing. A cat lay on its deck. Oonagh scooped it up and started hollering at once.

"O'Dea! O'Dea! Where you hiding yourself? It's not the rent man, you know."

From below came a man's voice. "Is it that wild girl come plaguing my rest again?"

These words were spoken with affection. Oonagh grinned and clumsily stroked the cat.

"Here I am. Here I am."

Man O'Dea appeared on deck. A wiry man with silver hair. He moved jerkily, feeling his way forward with massive spread hands. He wore boots without laces and his feet slopped about in them.

"Where's that brat?" he said, turning about him with exaggerated movements.

He reached out a hand. Oonagh went forward and stood beneath it. When Man brought it down, the girl held up the cat, so Man patted that instead of her. A gentleness came over his face as he understood the joke.

"My-my, Ooney-ooney, how soft your hair is getting. You must be washing it more these days."

Just then the cat let out a yowl and leapt down. Oonagh grumpily sucked her clawed hand. Man laughed and slapped his side. "How I love that cat," he said.

"Huh," sneered the girl.

"You have gone and got your friend?" asked Man.

Oonagh bristled with embarrassment. "She's not my friend. She's somebody I know."

"Ahh, but you'll be needing friends, Ooney-ooney," grinned Man, enjoying her discomfort. "You can't go hanging around with an old fellow for ever."

"Someone's got to."

Man laughed again. Stretching out his arm he said softly: "Where is she?"

Oonagh manœuvred Esther under Man's hand. This time, when his hand came down, it cupped Esther's head, gently tracing the outline of her features with its fingertips.

"A bonny girl," said Man. "Not like you, Ooney-ooney. Not the type to drink her whisky from a jam-jar. Is her voice just as sweet? What is your name, child?"

"Esther, if you please . . . sir," said Esther huskily.

"Sir! Sir! Why, there be no need to *sir* me, Esther."

"She doesn't know much," commented Oonagh, chewing on some bread and jam.

"Still, you've agreed to help Ooney-ooney tonight have you, child?"

"'Course she has!" said Oonagh before Esther could speak.

Man said: "Naturally I would go myself. But, as you no doubt have guessed, Esther, I am blind. In fact as blind as Moses Mummery himself," he chuckled, "who you tried to warn us against."

Oonagh couldn't meet Esther's eye. And Esther was far too shy to ask the manner of their secret business in front of O'Dea.

Oonagh dipped below. When she reappeared there was an old school satchel on her back. Esther was unable to restrain herself when she saw it.

"Hey!" she cried. "That's mine."

"*Was* yours," replied Oonagh. "You chucked it away. Remember? The Rats make use of cast-offs and stuff nobody else wants."

Man chuckled and nodded. However, Esther noticed his face grow gradually more serious. "You take care," he said. "Are you minding me, girl?"

"Yeh, I'm minding you."

"Then you go easy. Mad girl." The blind man chuckled affectionately and the cat purred in his lap.

The two girls left soon after. The reservoir was the colour of steel. Across it came the whispering murmurs of sleep with an occasional muttered word. Glancing back, Esther watched the bright lights of the house-boat slip away. Then, turning back, she noticed the satchel.

"What's in there?" she asked, tapping it with her foot.

Without ceasing to row, Oonagh said: "Dynamite."

Chapter Ten

"Wish I never told you now," said Oonagh sulkily. "Knew you'd only act like a stupid kid."

At first Oonagh had tried to reassure Esther with knowledgeable talk about detonators, charges, and electrical connections. Dynamite was virtually harmless on its own. Like putty. Besides, there was so little of it in the satchel, the worst it could do was blow a hand off, or so Oonagh insisted. But Esther was keen to retain both hands in place.

"Is that how he lost his sight?" asked Esther.

"Who?"

"Your fa – Man. Did Man O'Dea lose his sight in an explosion?"

The idea made Oonagh pause. They had reached the far side of the reservoir and she was tying the boat to a ring set into the metal-plated walls.

"Don't think so," she said. "Man doesn't tell how."

With Oonagh leading, they climbed into a pipe. It grew narrower until both girls went forward on hands and knees. When she rested to push her hair from her eyes, Esther could see the satchel waggling on the dumpy girl's back. Suppose it did go off. Suppose. Esther was quite good at the "suppose it should happen" game. Suppose . . . Oonagh was killed outright in a blinding flash and she had to go back and break the news to Man; of course he'd be heartbroken, but soon recover to adopt her in Oonagh's place. But suppose Oonagh was merely injured and she had to rescue her, paddling across the reservoir like a demon, with Oonagh murmuring: "Why Esther, I could never have rowed so fast." Sometimes Esther could make herself cry with her suppose games, even though an hour later she would scoff at her sentimentality.

"What are you thinking about?" asked Oonagh suspiciously.

"Oh!" said Esther, jumping. "Just about Zachary and Carl. They'll be so jealous when I tell them about this tomorrow."

"Huh!"

By now they were climbing a metal ladder

attached to the inside of a vertical pipe. Their feet chimed like bells at each rung.

"You haven't asked yet," said Oonagh.

"What about?"

"The dynamite."

"I suppose you're going to blow something up," shrugged Esther and Oonagh made an irritated noise.

Five minutes later they reached their destination. Esther could see no reason why this jumble of pipes was any different to similar ones passed on the way. Already Oonagh had emptied the contents of the satchel on the ground. She thrust something at Esther.

"Hold that," she said, gripping a screwdriver between her teeth.

Esther watched and did everything Oonagh told her. Soon they were unwinding wires down the length of the pipe.

Oonagh said: "Get running."

"What?"

"Scoot!"

"What about you?"

"Don't you worry yourself about me. I can out-run pretty girls like you."

Doubtfully Esther turned. She started to hurry away. Then quite unexpectedly the desire to prove herself took control. Bending down her head she forced herself to run like never before. Her feet rattled along the metal and oxygen pumped into her head making her dizzy with joy.

Somewhere over her shoulder came a sound like a distant firework.

"Run – run!" echoed an equally distant voice.

But Esther was tiring. And when foaming water washed over her feet, the shock almost stopped her in mid-stride.

"Run!" said the harsh voice behind her.

But running was quite impossible. The water was knee-deep and rising fast. It reached her waist. She fell forward and found herself swimming, the water cold, black and frothy. Then someone grabbed the scruff of her neck and yanked her to the base of a ladder.

"Climb!" shouted Oonagh.

Esther was coughing. She had swallowed water. She climbed slowly with Oonagh right behind. The further up they climbed the more dreadful sounded the water's roar below.

When the ladder ended, there was a door like a manhole cover. After they passed through it, Oonagh clanged it shut and bolted it down.

"You all right?" she asked.

Esther nodded. She was wringing out her cardigans.

A grin appeared across Oonagh's face. "Now the fun begins."

"Does it?" asked Esther doubtfully.

"Sure. Come see."

"But I'm tired and wet."

"C'mon! Stop whinging and behaving like a Miss Goody-Goody."

Once again they began to climb and crawl.

"Oh, where are we going, Oonagh?" wailed Esther, for she really was tired and shivering with cold.

"Shh!" whispered Oonagh. "We're right above Mr and Mrs Dunn's bedroom." She covered her mouth to stop a laugh escaping.

"Can we spy on them?" begged Esther.

"Lie on the floor. Feel for the watch-holes with your fingers, then lift them."

The floor – the reverse side of the Dunns' ceiling – was wooden with rafters running across it. The two girls squeezed themselves between them. It was dusty. Esther found a watch-hole first, her giggles annoying Oonagh until she found a watch-hole of her own. Soon both girls were enjoying the free peepshow together.

The Dunns' bed was set squarely beneath them. It was huge, with a post rising at each corner. Dunn was on his back, his mouth opening and closing with snores. Aphid was sitting up, looking bitter and poisonous. A shawl was draped around her shoulders and a nightlight flickered nearby.

She must have heard the girls giggle for under her breath she hissed the word, "Rats!" Then she spoke it again, louder, affirming the fact.

"R-ats!"

Her elbow dug away at Dunn's side like a miner's pick at a coal face.

"Eh? W-what is it, dearest?"

"Rats! Vermin! Sewer things! They're back. Look at me, Dunn. I'm a wreck. My hand is trembling. They haunt me. They seek me out. Just listen to them."

"You're a light sleeper, dearest," yawned Dunn, turning over and meaning to go straight back to sleep. But then a shriek arose from next door. "Now what?" he mumbled into his pillow.

"What is it, Miss Pursglove?" called Aphid shrilly.

As if in answer, the door crashed open and Miss Pursglove entered, born upon a wall of water. With her hair tightly enmeshed in curlers and face encased in a mud pack, together with the manner in which she flung herself upon the bed, Dunn must have thought a demented savage had come to cut his throat. He let out such a roar that even Aphid shrieked in response. Sobbing, Miss Pursglove lay across them both like a tiger-skin rug. In no time the water had risen on all sides. Brushes and slippers were floating upon it like little boats. And furniture, discovering buoyancy, began to shift and bump.

Leaping up, Aphid clenched her fists, screwed up her face and screamed: "I shall go mad!"

Chapter Eleven

Three days had passed. Now there was no water as well as no heat. Snow needed to be fetched and melted, yet sometimes the house was so cold it took hours to thaw. Aphid gave out the order to burn all old furniture. From room to room she stalked, condemning chairs and tables to the flames, and was so unapproachable that, when Carl became in need of a hair-cut, Esther decided to attempt it herself rather than tackle Mrs Dunn on the matter.

In the schoolroom Zachary chopped up Miss Frost's desk to make a blaze, while Esther got a sheet to wrap round Carl's neck. Each time, however, he prevented her.

"Don't be babyish, Carl," she said.

"You won't make me look stupid, Esther, will you, Esther?" he pleaded. "Cross your heart. I'll kill myself if people laugh at me because I look like a horrible convict."

"Of course they won't," said Esther crossly. "It'll be just the same as now but shorter. I bet nobody realizes."

Little by little she coaxed Carl on to Miss Frost's stool and quickly draped the sheet round him before he could change his mind. Frankie stood grinning as he held a mirror, catching in it Carl's sulky reflection.

Despite her words, Esther felt a little nervous. She took a comb and gently pulled it through Carl's hair which was marvellously thick and straight. For a while she found pleasure simply in grooming it. Combing it one way, then the other, and finally straight down over his eyes. Then she picked up the scissors.

"Hold still, Carl," she said. "Don't fidget or I'll snip your ear. No, I won't, silly. I was only joking. Now sit still or your fringe'll be crooked."

She didn't hear the door open.

"What, may I ask, is going on here?" demanded the cold voice.

Reflected in the mirror, Esther saw Mrs Dunn. Smiling grimly she advanced into the room and, holding the crown of Carl's head with her stare, encircled him with slow deliberate strides.

"Well? Who is going to tell me what mischief you're up to now?" she demanded. "Silence is a form of insolence too, you know."

"Not insolence, Mrs Dunn," stammered Esther. "It's a haircut. I mean, Carl's hair is getting so long I am cutting it for him."

"Are you indeed, miss?" glared Aphid. "You took it upon yourself to do so?" She held out her hand. "Give me those scissors. If you play with sharp implements you deserve to get cut."

Taking the scissors, Aphid paused, a wry smile spreading across her face. Slowly she reached out and snipped at Carl's fringe, seeming to take perverse pleasure from doing so. Then she froze, her hand pressed to her bosom.

"Gracious me! I saw something move! Something in that child's hair moved. I declare, he must be infested with lice. I distinctly saw it with my own eyes."

"I don't think – " began Esther.

Aphid swept her aside. "Give me that comb immediately, girl. You filthy, filthy children. Don't you know that if you live like animals, animals are what you become!"

So saying, she began hacking at Carl's hair with ever-increasing violence. "Esther!" he wailed, his hair dropping in clumps on the sheet before him. Aphid roughly angled his head this way and that, and the scissors snicked and snacked relentlessly until the task was done.

"There!" cried Aphid triumphantly, admiring her handiwork. "Dirt must be forced out wherever it's found."

Smiling grimly she swept from the room, whereupon Carl broke down in tears. Zachary and Esther ran forward but neither could comfort him. Even Frankie's own bottom lip trembled as he stood holding the mirror that reflected this miserable scene.

"Don't cry," said Zachary.

"She's just a witch," said Esther.

Jerking with sobs, Carl raised his eyes to view his red tear-stained face and cropped hair.

"She s-scalped me. That h-horrible, horrible f-fat poo-bag scalped me."

"It'll grow." Zachary tried to sound reassuring.

Carl only lowered his eyes again and his shoulders trembled. They thought he was crying. After a while they realized he was laughing. Laughing and crying together.

"She's scalped you!" shouted Zachary, and he and Esther started laughing too.

Then Zachary remembered. "Listen!" he called. "When I was smashing up Miss Frost's desk I found her make-up. Wait there, Carl."

He ran to the side of the room and snatched up a little bag. Wiping away Carl's tears with the flat of his hand, he began applying lipstick in bold stripes across the boy's forehead and cheeks.

"War-paint," he said. "Here, Esther, put it on me too. We'll be Indians. We'll always wear it because nobody ever takes notice of us. Today we declare war on Mrs Aphid Dunn, the queen of the palefaces. We are the last of the Mohicans and she is our sworn enemy!"

"Yaah! Death to grown-ups!" yelled Carl, leaping up and wrapping the sheet around him like a cape. "Let's scalp 'em and eat 'em."

Zachary painted the war colours on Esther and a less-than-happy Frankie. Then they joined together in a fierce war-dance around the schoolroom. They whooped and held up burning pieces of Miss Frost's desk. Carl wrote rude things on the blackboard, and they chanted to the wolf-god to revenge their tribe.

Suddenly Zachary broke away and ran to the window. He did so with such urgency that the others stood still watching him.

"What is it?" asked Carl, slowly pulling the sheet from off his head.

Zachary said: "Blackhead has just ridden from the trees, and he isn't alone."

Perhaps they were imagining it, but from that moment a change came over the house. Zachary said it was the aura of evil. Esther told him to shut up. He was frightening her and she didn't know what aura meant.

Occasionally feet were heard pattering past the schoolroom. The news was spreading amongst the servants. Esther wondered if the Rats had heard too.

Suddenly Carl said: "I feel sick."

★

For the remainder of that day the children lurked about their schoolroom, gloomily burning picture books and atlases. They acted as if in a state of siege; the approach of footsteps breaking off their whispered conversations, and imagining noises behind the walls.

The younger ones turned to Zachary for leadership, for without a vote or a single word he had become their elected chief, silently proclaiming himself as such by the two quills in his hair. Moreover, he had the book – the book about Indians, which was suddenly their guide to survival. He sat on Miss Frost's stool with the three others squatting on the floor before him. "We have to learn to protect ourselves," he said, holding open the book at a page illustrated with tomahawks.

The others nodded vigorously.

"I'm going to bed with my penknife under my pillow," said Carl.

Zachary shut the book and frowned. "But that wouldn't be any use against Moses Mummery. He's a vampire. We need things like garlic."

"But where can we get garlic?" asked Esther. "You know that the master hated it. Remember that time he smelt it on a footman's breath?"

Zachary pushed his unchiefly specs up his nose. Looking around the schoolroom he noticed for the first time how incredibly bare it was.

"If we hadn't burnt the rulers," said Carl, "we

could have made signs of the cross."

"But he's blind," said Zachary.

"Anyway we *have* burnt the rulers," said Esther. "We burnt them days ago because we all hate measuring."

On the floor – it used to stand on Miss Frost's desk – was a porcelain clock. It had a little figure with books under its arm, tilted forward as if running. On the other side of the dial was a larger figure with a mortar-board and cane. Underneath was written: A PUNCTUAL CHILD IS A VIRTUOUS CHILD.

"Soon be dinner time," said Zachary. "I suppose we'll meet him then."

Usually the children looked upon dinner time with mixed feelings. The dining-room was bright and warm. Coming up a corridor of dingy gas-mantles, the double doors would open on to a room flooded with candle-light and fire; the silver and gilt alive, as only they can be, beneath real flame. If they could simply enjoy these pleasures alone. But it meant suffering the company of Mrs Dunn and the nervous twitterings of Miss Pursglove, and Dunn who, these days, was gloomy and morose. Blackhead, unctuous and oily, was there to serve, wearing his false smile like a thief in his mask. Yet these things the children could tolerate for the luxury of their only hot meal of the day.

However, that night, the four would have gladly gone cold and hungry. They shuffled up the dim corridor beneath the disapproving stares of the portraits. Then the doors parted. The people at the table looked up.

"You're late!" said Aphid coldly. "Don't you ill-mannered children ever do anything to please your elders? And can't you see we have a special visitor tonight?"

Oh yes, they saw. They saw . . . They stood staring at him. Frozen. Unable to move.

"Well!" snapped Aphid. "Have we to wait all evening? Get yourselves seated."

At this Carl began to cry.

"What's wrong with him?" demanded Mrs Dunn.

"He's been a little poorly today," replied Esther meekly.

Dunn looked up as if waking from a dream. "Unwell eh, Master Carl? Come sit by me. I'll take care of y—"

"Don't you pamper that child no more, Dunn. They're over-pampered as it is. Spoilt. That's their trouble. Spoilt beyond belief."

Dunn slipped back into his stupor. Was there nothing left he could do?

The children edged round to their places. They couldn't take their eyes off Moses Mummery.

He smiled towards them. A thin reptilian smile. And curiously, unlike other blind people, he always looked where he should be looking, as if really sighted. Whenever anyone spoke, he tilted his head towards the speaker, an expression of polite interest on his face.

It was hard to judge, but he must have been seventy, with the mottled markings of old age upon his forehead. His hair, so fine, was scraped back to reveal a raw pink scalp. His face, small and pinched, was almost bird-like; not unpleasant in itself, but somehow bewitching. His hands were wondrously long and still elegantly formed. He wore dark clothing, except for a sash which crossed his chest diagonally. This was the colour of blood.

"Master Mummery," said Aphid, speaking abruptly. "You are not eating."

Mummery smiled. His teeth were small and pointed. "Please. Be good enough to excuse me, Mrs Dunn. My appetite is small. I am like a sparrow. Happy to peck a few crumbs."

His voice caused the children to stop eating and openly stare at him. It was like a rasping whisper. Esther saw that Miss Pursglove was shaking. The overdone pearls and lace that started at her head and ended at her ankles trembled like foliage. She constantly dabbed her mouth.

Mummery turned to Aphid, his eyes bright but unfocused.

"Surrounded by such beautiful things," he

said in his soft growl. "Believe me, once I lived as you do, Mrs Dunn. But in my life my fortunes have been mixed. Now I am pleased to rely on charitable strangers like yourself."

He sipped his red wine, chasing the taste along his bottom gum with his tongue. His lips were stained red. When he put down the glass it looked like blood around his mouth. He fondled the crystalware before him and ran his fingers around the patterned rim of his plate. He was not at all clumsy.

"Exquisite," he said softly, almost in a sob.

Forgetting herself Esther blurted out, "But how can you see these things when you are b—"

"Blind!" He smiled. "Esther, isn't it?" His voice was a low purr. "Why, I see with my fingers, dear Esther. To me gold leaf is as thick as a rug."

Aphid was frowning. "How dare you be rude to our guest, girl!" she snarled. "Pursglove! Write down this child's name at once and deduct a potato from her next meal."

Poor Miss Pursglove was trembling so much that all she could do was write a line of scribble.

After dinner, a treat. Crisply Aphid announced it, then Blackhead swept the dinner things away with a silent efficiency that was becoming his hallmark. He guided the assembled company to the scarlet sofas and frowned at the under-servants as the room was re-arranged. Their dining seats were set in rows and a small table positioned behind them. Upon it was placed a magic lantern.

Like a sleep-walker, Moses Mummery went forward, his arms outstretched, until they brushed the old machine. Then he embraced it, his fingers lovingly stroking the metal.

"Please, ladies, gentlemen, and children too, of course," he said in a husky whisper. "Please take up your places." And when the sounds of shuffling and throat clearing had died away, he added: "Would someone be kind enough to extinguish the lights."

Blackhead smoothly slid to comply. Darkness. Through it Esther could hear the old man breathing.

At once a dusty beam of light fell upon a screen. Metal scraped against metal, and the first slide was jerked into place. A group of people had appeared in tones of browns and faded yellows: ladies in long dresses and a stern seated gentleman unflinchingly regarding his audience as once he had the photographer. He looked vaguely familiar. Then Esther noticed that one of the ladies was holding a bundle draped in a lacy shawl. It was a baby. It was Mummery himself: baby Mummery, with his proud parents and doting aunts. Esther felt herself grow cold. Once this dreadful old man had been a small baby. The idea appalled her.

There followed a succession of sepia-coloured views of the past. India: elephants and tea with a maharajah; turbaned servants, tiger hunts and vultures around a water hole.

Stumblingly, Mummery tried to explain each image. He sounded wistful and sad, even though he could not see what his audience saw. Too much drink, however, had caused Dunn to slump down in his seat. He snored loudly. Miss Pursglove had slipped away as soon as the lights had dimmed; and Aphid knitted furiously, not paying the slightest attention to the screen. Only the children watched. They watched in fascinated horror. They knew the destiny of that serious-faced, podgy little boy, pictured with his toy horse and Indian nurse.

Then, like a nightmare, a great devouring shadow bore down upon the children. Frankie gave a startled cry. Only afterwards did they realize that Mummery had accidentally crossed in front of the magic lantern.

"So sorry," he hissed. "So very sorry."

Chapter Twelve

And so Moses Mummery became part of the household at the big house. Aphid allowed him a box-room next to the library with a permanent fire glowing in its grate for, as she said, old men die of the cold and she didn't want the expense and trouble of Mummery's body before he had done his work and rid the house of its vermin. To this end she had every map and blueprint of the drains brought to Mummery, who was to be seen poring over them by the light of a single candle.

The children watched him through the glass panels in the library door and the door to his den. Before he came, they had liked to play in the library, making nests and look-outs from the master's great and rare volumes, climbing the carved mahogany shelves like mountaineers. Not now, however. Now they whispered together in the dimly-lit corridor outside; and if Frankie grew too excited, or made a noise, Carl quickly thrust a hand across his mouth.

Zachary frowned. "How can he read?" he said. "How on earth can he possibly see to read?"

Carl's eyes were fixed, as if mesmerized, to Mummery's single candle. "He can't. He feels the writing."

"With his fingers?"

"That's what he told Mrs Dunn," said Carl, his eyes still held by the tiny light. "He told her he can feel a difference between the paper and the ink; he can follow the scratches people make with pen nibs, too."

Esther shivered, pulling the old blanket that made her look like a squaw closely about her. "This whole side of the house smells of *him*," she observed distastefully.

The others nodded. It was not an unpleasant smell. Like musty violets, sweet, yet decaying. Wafting on the old man's breath whenever he spoke. Yet in the grip of winter the odour was unnatural. Esther shivered again. Aura of evil – the phrase had haunted her since first hearing it. She still didn't know what it meant, but was sure it was the smell of violets.

As they watched, Moses constantly rose and entered the library, only to return to his den with a book, chosen by a light touch of its spine. But suddenly he was no longer amongst the books but fast approaching the door to the corridor.

"He's coming out," whispered Esther. "Let's run. Please, let's run!"

"Shhh. No time," hissed Zachary. "Stand back against the wall. He's blind. He's bound to walk right by us."

As they stepped back against the wall, the library door opened. The smell of violets intensified. In the corridor, Mummery fumbled for his key before finally fishing out a large bunch. He was feeling for the lock with his fingertips when, seemingly, he sniffed the air and sensed something. Hurriedly he locked the door, thrust the keys into his pocket and spun around.

"Who's there?" he called harshly.

Esther could hear her heart thudding.

"I said who's there? Speak or you'll be sorry you don't."

"Please—"

"Children? Is it the children?"

The shadow disappeared from Mummery's face. He held out his arms as if embracing them.

"The children. Do not be afraid. Please excuse me if I frighten you. I walk in darkness, you see, it makes me apprehensive of the slightest thing. Come forward. Do not be afraid. I am your friend."

They shuffled a step closer. Mummery's hand accidentally touched Carl's cheek.

"Ah. Such soft skin. It must be Esther."

"Carl," said the boy darkly.

"Ah, Carl. And this fine fellow must be Zachary." Mummery's hand cupped Zachary's neck, moving to his shoulders and sliding down his arms.

"You will make an excellent soldier," said Mummery with a laugh.

"Don't want to be a soldier," mumbled Zachary. But Mummery wasn't listening. He had found Esther, his fingers stroking her hair, forcing her to remember the other blind man. Man O'Dea. That time she hadn't minded him touching her. She was tense as the hot scent of violets came gushing over her face.

Then something quite strange occurred. Mummery's hand brushed Frankie. Fear and pain crossed the old man's face and he leapt back as if scalded. Frankie, as puzzled as the others, smiled innocently at him.

"I – I must go now," said Mummery, a little shaken. "But do come and see me again. I shall look forward to having you visit me. Now goodbye. Goodbye."

He hurried away and Zachary said: "Let's track the paleface down and see where he goes."

Shadowing Mummery was easy, even at a distance. Not only was he slow (and blind of course), but the smell of violets kept them upon his trail, even when he entered one of the master's forbidden rooms. Once inside they rushed to the key-hole to spy on him.

The key-hole was one of those big old-fashioned brass types, enabling them to watch two at a time. Beyond the door lay the master's orchid room, although the cold had withered most orchids, turning them brown. The fleshy, gaudy flowers remaining were tight shell-like ears and between them and the rows of dead and dying blooms prowled a figure. It was Blackhead. As he walked, he nervously pulled apart a flower that he held pinched between his fingers. The musty smell of violets announced his visitor and he paused.

"Blackhead?" breathed Mummery hoarsely. "Are you there, boy?"

"I'm here," replied Blackhead in a surly voice. "And I ain't no boy."

The old man chuckled indulgently. "As you please. But I doubt whether you've been shaving for many years."

Angrily Blackhead touched the fine fluff above his top lip that he was too embarrassed to shave off.

"Yes," continued Mummery. "I believe the gulf between our ages is considerable."

Blackhead plucked the last petals from the flower and threw it down. "Listen, old man," he said, "the only difference between us is our pasts.

Yours, Mr Mummery, is quite a dark 'istory. Or so I'm led to believe."

Mummery visibly winced. In a whisper he said: "And don't you think that I would change it if I could? Don't hurry to align yourself with evil, Blackhead. There can never be any turning back. It is like an illness that takes hold and eats away at you from the inside."

Blackhead coughed.

"Are you unwell?" Mummery turned to him with genuine concern. "Think on what I have just told you," he said.

"It's just a cough, old man. I had to fetch you in the cold. Remember?"

Mummery sighed heavily and propped himself against a ledge, the dead orchids surrounding him. "Tell me why you have sent for me," he said.

"I need you to help me," began Blackhead, as he paced up and down like the caged wolf that the foresters had once brought to show the children. "There's things I want. This house, its lands. Ain't much to ask, eh, Mr Mummery? But I've got brains and I'm young and clever enough to get what I want. I want folk to respect me, call me *Mr* Blackhead. Sir. I want power. And ain't that what it's all about, Mr Mummery? Power. And I'll tell you summat else for nothing, I'm sick of waiting table on a booby like Dunn and the rest of the ninnies."

"So how can I help?"

"It's the wife, Mrs Dunn."

"Ahh, our charming hostess."

"Charming?" said Blackhead darkly. "You don't need eyes to suss that one out. Charming, her? I hate her, Mr Mummery. She thinks she'll get what she wants from me by bending me round her little finger like that mad 'usband of 'ern. Not me. Not me, Mr Mummery. I work alone. I'd sooner cut that uns' throat than dance her tune."

"But what can I do?"

"Distract her. Keep her away from me. Report on what she does. I wouldn't put forging the master's will in her favour beyond that 'un."

"And my own reward?"

"Why," said Blackhead, suddenly stopping in his tracks. "I'll be your apprentice, Mr Mummery. A very good one I'll be too."

Mummery snorted. "What nonsense is this? You talk as if I offer you a trade. Apprentice to what, eh, Blackhead?"

"Why, Mr Mummery," smiled Blackhead, "to evil, of course."

Chapter Thirteen

They met Leah the French maid on their way to dinner. She stood at the bottom of the staircase, surrounded by battered suitcases and hat-boxes. The little lace handkerchief clenched to her face hardly appeared adequate for the tears. She kissed each child goodbye.

"Ah, your adorable little faces. So sweet. So trusting. But what is that that covers them?"

"Lipsti—" began Carl.

"War-paint," corrected Zachary.

"We're the last of the mohairs."

"Mohicans!"

"We're on the war-path," Carl explained. "Against the great paleface queen – and Spotty Face – and Pursglove person. I suppose Mr Dunn too. We still quite like him, although he drinks too much fire-water."

Leah clasped them in her arms. "Truly, I wish I could 'ug you up and take you with me. I am going 'ome to Clermont-Ferrand. I 'ave written to Mama and she is preparing my old room looking out across the sea. Papa 'as a lighthouse. I cannot stay a moment longer under the same roof as that Monsieur Mummery. Truly I cannot. When the steam-sledge is ready I am gone."

She kissed them again.

With her head bent forward she said in a whisper: "You know what they are saying about 'im? They say that he must 'ave living creatures brought to 'im at night – and they are never seen alive again. Never! Next day their poor little bodies are found, sucked dry of every drop of blood."

"No!" cried the outraged children. "Who told you this?"

Leah waved her handkerchief at them. "I am not at liberty to say," she sniffed. "But listen to me and listen well. Do not go alone with that old man. Truly he is dangerous. And 'e 'as a reputation the Devil 'imself would envy."

They left her to weep amongst her luggage. Carl too began to cry.

"Stop crying, you big baby!" snapped Esther. "You know how Leah loves to spin a yarn. Some say she isn't even French at all."

"Not crying," he murmured. "Got something in my eye."

But, in truth, each one was holding back the tears. Each one was as frightened as the other. Even Frankie, who understood little but keenly sensed their fears.

Then the double doors at the end of the long dark corridor swung open and all was shining and all was bright, as if nothing was wrong in the house. The adults sat talking around the table. Blackhead bowed low. But now Esther only saw his mask. He hates me, she thought, he hates every one of us here.

During the course of dinner, the children only had eyes for Moses Mummery. They watched what he ate. But he didn't eat at all. He drank his blood-red wine or had Blackhead fetch him lukewarm water, which he sipped constantly.

Nor was he the only one lacking an appetite. Dunn hardly touched a thing on his plate. He had lost weight and looked ill. His clothes hung loose upon him, as if belonging to another. Every now and again his eyes would flit about the table as if seeking something to do. Once he rose to fetch another bottle of wine and Aphid said in a firm voice: "Blackhead. Please be kind enough to bring Mr Dunn another bottle of claret." And she shot her husband the look usually reserved for the children. Esther tried to catch his eye or to smile at him. But he didn't seem real any more; he was more like a ghost.

Aphid helped herself to more beef. She said

to Mummery: "Miss Pursglove was asking how soon it would be before you rid the house of its rats, Mr Mummery?"

"She was?" hissed Mummery, fixing his blind eyes upon Miss Pursglove.

"W-was I?" quaked Miss Pursglove.

"You were, dear. You were," smiled Aphid, her thin lips pulled tight. A tacit agreement existed between Mummery and Aphid to trouble poor Miss Pursglove as often as they could. She was more frightened of the old man than anyone. Her nerves were in a frenzy if he so much as spoke her name.

"Well, Miss Pursglove," growled Mummery softly. "I have studied all the plans most carefully. I intend to enter the sewers and begin my work tomorrow."

A knife dropped heavily on a plate. Mummery cocked his head as if listening. "Who was that?" he asked, all the sharp little teeth in his mouth revealed.

"One of those clumsy children," replied Aphid frowning.

"Ah, that reminds me," continued Mummery. "I was going to ask if I might have permission for the children to help me tomorrow. Oh, it will not be hard work, you understand. But a blind man sometimes needs the assistance of those gifted with sight."

"Take 'em all," said Aphid, her mouth full of

food. "They do nothing but hang about the house all day."

Just then Esther caught Dunn's eye. He had the look of a dog beaten into submission.

Beyond midnight. Silently, a caped figure moved down the corridors, a candle lighting the way. At the library it stopped to pull a key from a pocket. The locked door clicked and the hooded person entered, gliding past the black ranks of books towards the tiny box-room. Its door was open. Moses Mummery sat by his glowing fire. He looked up, his blind eyes white and shining.

"Will you sit?" he asked.

The figure pulled down the hood. It was Aphid Dunn.

"No."

"Well?"

"I have brought the money like I promised." She held out a heavy bag. "Do you want to count it?"

He shook his head. "Money means little to me now," he said. "Leave it by the bed."

He heard the bag thud as she dropped it.

"Do you wish to know how it is to be done?"

"No," she said firmly.

"It will be painless."

Her face in the firelight turned hard. She said: "Mr Mummery, children are dying all around the world. They are not known by, or of any interest to, me. I want it so with the four who live under this roof. All I ask is that it looks like an accident."

He nodded again. Bending, he prodded the embers. When he straightened up, Aphid had gone. The door was just clicking behind her.

At once Mummery's face altered. It grew twisted with pain. Clutching his chest, he dropped to his knees.

"Why must evil be heaped upon me?" he cried. "Why can't others have their share of the burden? Why?"

Chapter Fourteen

That same night Esther, Zachary and Carl held a pow-wow. (Frankie was left to sleep, he'd only get over-excited and spoil things.) The meeting was held in Zachary's bed. A small table had been lugged beneath the covers, whereupon its single leg became the upright to the wigwam it formed. A night-light lit the interior; and the three children settled down cross-legged to discuss what should be done, come the morning.

Should they run away?

Hide?

Beg the Rats for help?

"Whatever happens," said Zachary, "Indian braves never let each other down."

The two others nodded enthusiastically. Then Carl yawned. It was very late.

Zachary pushed his glasses up his nose and

opened his book. He said: "True Indians always pledge their loyalty, and this becomes a lasting bond that not even death and the grave can break."

Carl and Esther looked at him. Esther wanted to laugh, as she always did when Zachary was serious. She bit her lip and he continued: "If we mix our blood together, as the Indians did, we shall be blood brothers, and by our deeds and by our blood we shall become as one."

At this Carl and Esther raised violent objections. Eventually Carl consented to let Zachary prick his thumb. But Esther stubbornly held out against them, refusing to mingle her blood with anybody's if it meant cutting or pricking.

In the end, a compromise. Fetching a spoon from his cocoa mug, Zachary licked it and passed it on to Carl, who likewise licked it and passed it on to Esther. Pulling a face, she touched the spoon with the tip of her tongue, as if it had been used to measure a deadly poison. For a second time Zachary and Carl licked it.

Closing his eyes, Zachary began to chant: "By our spit have we become brothers—"

"And sisters," added Esther.

"And sisters," agreed Zachary.

"I know," piped up Carl. "If we give Frankie this spoon at breakfast, he'll become our spit-brother too, without realizing it."

Just then someone grabbed hold of the

blankets at the bottom of the bed and yanked them violently. A rush of air extinguished the night-light. The table leaned, then toppled over, and the three squawking children fought a tangle of bed-clothes to be free.

Was it Aphid, Mummery or Dunn? The hooting laughter answered that. It was none of them.

Poking his head from the sheets, Zachary made out the figure of Oonagh, her hands on her hips and her body convulsed with amusement.

"That wasn't very funny," he said.

"Wasn't meant to be." She wiped away the tears of laughter. "But if you could only hear how stupid you sound."

Zachary lit a candle as Carl babbled on excitedly, telling Oonagh about Mummery's plan to invade the Rats' domain.

"Oonagh'll know about that already," said Esther. "She'd have heard The Whispers."

"Can't say I have," shrugged Oonagh. She sat on the edge of the bed and, slipping her hands behind her head, fell back across the quilt, as if a bed was an unheard-of luxury. "Been on a mission for the Rats. Up in the lofts. Total waste of time if you ask me. But then they're up to something."

"Who?" asked Carl, climbing on to the bed beside her.

"The Rats. They're having top secret meetings. Like *yours*." She laughed again. "And every Rat has to attend."

"So why don't *you*?" asked Zachary.

Oonagh pulled a face. "Because I'm not a true Rat. I'm a found thing. Something Man O'Dea fished up."

She grew sombre for a while. Then, leaping up, she cried: "But you've never been on the roof of this place before? I tell you it could be the top of the world, the snow's that deep. How about coming to see for yourselves?"

Tired as they were, they clamoured at the chance.

In a single bounce, Oonagh landed next to the window-seat. The three others followed her into it: Esther, Carl, and finally Zachary who closed the seat behind him. Esther thought she might remember the way, but somewhere Oonagh took a different turning. Soon they were climbing the inside of a ventilation pipe. It had rungs conveniently welded to the smooth metal, and went up and up as straight as a pillar.

They emerged into night and snow, their laughter turning to clouds of steam.

Straight away the boys went off on their own to explore, sliding down roofs and shinning up the sooty chimney-stacks that pierced many of the tiled slopes like monstrous candy sticks. At the clock tower Carl clambered on to Zachary's shoulders to push the minute hand to twelve.

Immediately the clock started to rumble, booming out three times across the silent countryside, forcing the boys to crouch down with their hands over their ears, while their giggles went unheard.

"Hey, Esther!" they called. "What are you doing?"

Esther looked up to smile but didn't reply. She busied herself by brushing snow off the stone lions that guarded the parapet. To her they looked so pitiful, snowbound and fettered in ice. Glancing up again, she noticed Oonagh grinning at her in an indulgent way.

"They're not real lions, you know," she said.

Soon the boys were creating more noise, hurling snow at each other. However, when they heard a wolf's banshee-like howl, they drew close to Esther and all three peered silently down into the gardens. Far below the snow was grey. Upon it, black shapes endlessly encircled each other, and from the forest poured more wolves in dark bands, each about a dozen strong.

"Poor things are hungry," said Esther. "The winter's been hard on them."

"But why are they here at all?" said Zachary.

"They're waiting," replied Oonagh, with all the smugness of one who knows.

Before they could press her further, light fell across the wolves. They rose snarling as, into the bright patch made by an open door directly below, a figure crept, crouched and barely human. He was clad in a wolf-skin, the wolf's head fitting him like a cap. It was Zachary's hand-painted picture come to life – the one entitled *Braves out hunting*. Clearly the wolf-pack honoured him as pure wolf and Esther, who couldn't get Zachary's book from her mind, felt the world reel about her.

"It's Blackhead!" she heard Zachary whisper. "See, it's Blackhead!"

"He's king of the wolves," said Carl excitedly.

As they watched, Blackhead approached the wolves, moving in a curiously animal-like way. The wolves, baying all around him, only fell silent when the youth began casting food in all directions. Hungrily the wolves fell upon it. Snarling, fighting each other, running away trailing strings of sausages. In their frenzy, wolves brushed against Blackhead, leaping up like powerful dogs, but not hurting him. When the food was gone Blackhead slowly backed away leaving the wolves to run wild across the snow-bound lawns. The patch of light vanished abruptly as the door closed. It was done.

"They didn't eat him!" cried Carl disappointedly, his shrill voice breaking the silence. "They didn't eat horrible old spotty face."

"But I don't understand," said Esther. "What is Blackhead trying to do?"

"It's simple," said Oonagh. "He's winning the wolves' trust. Of course he'll never tame them completely, but they can be trained."

"But why?"

"What better way is there of ridding the house of your rivals than having them eaten by wild beasts?"

"You silly," smiled Esther. "How will the wolves get into the house in the first place?"

Oonagh threw back her head and laughed. "That's as easy as blowing up a pipe. You simply leave the doors open."

Suddenly Esther remembered the snow-bound parlour. "I want to go back to bed," she said. "I'm cold."

"Bed!" scoffed Oonagh. "What, now? I haven't shown you the other treat yet. Come on, follow me."

She led the way up and down the slated roofs and along the heavy leaded guttering, on which icicles hung, as big as dinosaur claws.

"This is the place," she said at last. She had stopped by a skylight, the shape of a glass tent. They crouched down, each one clearing a peep-hole in the snow.

The room below was recognized at once.

"It's our old nursery!" exclaimed Esther. "Where we used to go with Nanny Meekins."

"And Dunn used to come and show us tricks, and we would have to guess the pocket he hid our sweets in," added Carl.

From this unfamiliar angle they viewed the

room that once had almost been the limit of their world. The shelves of toys, the camp beds for afternoon naps, the miniature tables and chairs. Plus, of course, Nanny Meekins' old wicker seat where she would sit, begging the children for less noise while she enjoyed forty winks. But gradually the room had grown less and less important. Too babyish. And with a hundred other rooms to explore, it was never visited again.

"Look!" said Carl. "See who it is?"

They did indeed. It was Dunn, yet the shadow of the Dunn they had known. Oonagh beamed triumphantly at them and kept slyly regarding their expressions for any signs of change.

For a while the old butler paced from wall to wall – removing his bowler, putting it on again, mopping his brow, and straightening his tie. And, wandering along the shelves, he took down toys, hugging them to him, squeezing them tightly in his arms.

Then his mood changed abruptly. He raced across the room to the rocking-horse and clambered upon it, his body ridiculously large on that small wooden toy. As he swung it into life, Carl and Zachary sniggered. Oonagh grinned at Esther, but she turned away.

Dunn's face grew wilder and wilder as the rocking of the horse became more and more violent. Harsh shadows whipped to and fro.

They could hear the creak of wood. To and fro. To and fro. Until, at last, he ceased to rock and gradually rode the horse to a standstill. Sitting pale and upright in the saddle, his hands cradled his head.

"He's done the same for the past five nights now," said Oonagh.

Esther found her vision blurred. Her tears melted the snow.

Chapter Fifteen

When they returned to their big damp beds there lingered with each child a vague feeling that, come the morning, nothing would be left to fear. It was like a taste in their mouths. The Rats would save them or at least prevent them from coming to any harm. But against this were a number of pressing doubts that were pushed to the backs of their minds. Why hadn't the Rats acted before now? And Oonagh's smiling assurances could count as nothing. Why, the Rats didn't even include her as one of their number. She was an outsider. How could she possibly speak for them?

Awakening to the grey light of dawn, Esther could not taste the hope any more, and the leadenness in her stomach had grown. She leapt from her bed. She would run to the boys. They would escape and—

And nothing. Just then the door opened and Miss Pursglove entered, stooping her head like a giraffe although a good two feet of air existed between her severely-bunned hair and the lintel. She frowned as she saw Esther's face drop.

"M-Miss Pursglove!"

"What is the matter with you, child?"

"I-I didn't expect you. That's all."

As Esther gazed on Miss Pursglove's face, a remarkable change took place there. It was as if her features had become a battleground. It started with the mouth. The two unnaturally taut lips began to twitch, almost imperceptibly at first, at either corner, until gradually the tremor claimed the entire length of bottom lip. Then it was the turn of the eyes. As if sending messages in Morse code, they began to blink. And by the time the tears were rolling, both nostrils had joined in the hostilities too. First they were circles, then they were slits as she sucked up air and exhaled it again. Miss Millicent Pursglove became convulsed by sobs.

Rushing to her, Esther placed an arm about her bony hips and guided her to the bed where she sat down.

"How s-silly of me," sniffed Miss Pursglove. "But it's just . . . well, it's just . . . just that Mrs Dunn has sent me to take you to that wretched Mummery man. And the truth is he t-terrifies me half out of my wits!"

Esther climbed upon the bed, putting an arm around the woman's trembling shoulders.

"Well, then it's easy, Miss Pursglove," she whispered into her ear. "Don't take us to him. Say you forgot. Or couldn't find us."

"Don't be so silly, child," said Miss Pursglove briskly, regaining her composure and rising off the bed like a stick balancing a china plate. "Why, these days even Mrs Dunn fills me with dread. It's this awful house. This awful rat-infested house."

In the schoolroom, Carl's hair still lay on the floor. They toyed with it, with the toes of their shoes. Mournful glances were exchanged, but nobody spoke.

Miss Pursglove's lather was unabated. Esther noticed that a strand of hair had worked free of the immaculate bun on top of her head. It was as she was fretting with her collar that she suddenly let out a shrill inexplicable scream.

"Look! See what you have caused me to do," she cried accusingly.

Four sullen faces confronted her, eyes dipping a moment to view the tiny red pearl on the finger pricked by the brooch.

"That vampire'll smell the blood on me," she wailed. "He'll be like a shark. A terrible smiling shark."

Carl bared his teeth at her. "Grrrrr," he purred like a tiger.

Grabbing his collar, Miss Pursglove frog-marched him through the door, his toes barely touching the ground. The three others followed, with Frankie pulling puzzled faces as if practising how to be bewildered.

They saw him at once, seated at the far end of the long corridor. At the same time, the sickly scent of violets became powerfully strong. Miss Pursglove faltered like a wounded gazelle, then continued her approach with purposeful strides.

Carl whispered to Esther. "Look at him, Esther. He's got a cat. One of the kitchen mousers, and he's stroking it!"

"Shh," hissed Esther, her expression unaltering.

Carl said: "Remember what Leah told us? Do you remember, Esther?"

"Shhhh!"

"Those small animals that were never seen alive again. Every bit of blood squeezed out of them like an orange."

"Oh please don't, Carl . . . Carl!"

But Carl had gone bounding down the corridor. When he reached Mummery his hand fell in a swiping motion. Defensively the cat lashed out too. As it streaked away into the distance, Carl gazed down at his scratched and bleeding wrist.

"There, Mr Mummery!" said Miss Pursglove

triumphantly. "Upon that child is *fresh* blood."

With these words she delivered her charges and disappeared up the corridor with barely less haste, or grace, than the cat.

"Good morning, good morning," said Mummery. "Are you well? Did you sleep well? Good, good . . ." He spoke breathlessly, not waiting for a reply, which, in any case, never came. He chose to make nothing of the cat incident; it seemed to have been instantly forgotten.

The children were drawn to his eyes, which were extraordinarily bright, but calm. They seemed to calm the children too, as if hypnotic. Otherwise, Mummery appeared possessed by a nervous energy. He spoke rapidly but of nothing in particular.

After a few minutes Zachary noticed the dagger at the old man's side, in a scabbard of peeling leather. He touched it.

"But, Mr Mummery," he cried, "shouldn't we protect ourselves too?"

Mummery laughed, showing all his pointed teeth but not making a sound. "What? Children arm themselves? Be given knives? What next? Knives are sharp. You'll go hurting yourselves. Besides we only need one knife between us. Rest assured, I know how to use it. Now we have work to do. See, I have opened the hatch here. We must descend. Into the dark with you. Ladies first, dear Esther. Ladies first. What, afraid? But what is there to be afraid of? The dark? Why, I have grown quite used to it these last twenty years."

Using his hypnotic charm, Mummery eased them down the metal rungs of a ladder. He followed last, reaching out to drag the iron door to.

"No!" shouted Zachary.

Mummery wheezed. "My dear young soldier," he said hoarsely. "We can't have those terrible vicious sewer things escaping into the main part of the house, can we now? Imagine poor Mrs Dunn. And see, things aren't so bad. In my pocket – four candles. One for each of you. Yes, yes. Light them. It's your own light for the darkness."

The old man's voice had acquired a vibrant, tinny edge. The smell of sweet violets swirled about him, filling the tunnel where they stood.

"Lead on," he rasped. "And tell me at once if you see any sign of Mrs Dunn's rats. Their eyes'll glow in the light of your candles. Don't be afraid. They'll be more afraid of you. Everything is afraid of something else."

For many minutes they walked along the tunnel until they reached a large empty tank. Its entrance was a circular hatchway. Mummery didn't seem at all surprised when it was announced.

"Boys," he said. "Be good boys. Go down and check that it is empty."

The boys hesitated. But Mummery had some kind of power in him. It glowed softly through his eyes. It met the candle-light with a light of its own. It could not be resisted.

Carl climbed down first. Then Zachary, who helped Frankie. As he descended into the darkness, Frankie looked helplessly at Esther, appealing to her with his eyes. But she could find no words to say to him. Nothing at all.

Mummery cocked his head. When he could hear three sets of feet on the tank's metal floor, he pushed the hatch shut and secured it down.

In his blindness, his hand searched the air. When it met Esther's wrist it became confident, the long fingers gripping it securely.

"Come, Esther," he said in a whisper, so close to her face that she could taste the violets. "Come walk with me. Just a little further. A little way further, my dear."

The boys awoke as if from a dream. They came to their senses as they heard the rumble. It sounded like a steam train thundering towards them down a tunnel and came from a pipe that jutted into the tank quite close to its metal roof. The rumble came again, a spurt of water suddenly shooting from the pipe. Then another. Then a dribble of water, the dribble becoming a flow, becoming a jet. The boys were splashing in it ankle-deep before they reached the metal rungs that only led back to the locked hatch.

Slowly the swirling black water chased them up the ladder. Their cries were useless and, in any case, quite drowned out by the roar.

Chapter Sixteen

"Come along, Esther. Step lively, dear. You're dragging your heels. Are you tired? Are you weary?"

"No," replied Esther miserably. She felt crushed beneath Mummery's brightness. His eyes shone and his hand burned in hers.

"Do you see them? Do you see those abominable rats? Hold up your candle, dear. Hold it up. Do their wicked eyes glint back at you?" He chuckled.

"No."

"They will. They will."

He chuckled again.

They walked in silence, in a perfumed cloud of violets.

"I will cheer you up, Esther dear," said Mummery. "I will recite a poem. It is from a book,

Esther. A book about a sweet little girl like you."

"Does she die at the end?" asked Esther.

The old man chuckled wheezily. Then he began to recite, his voice dry and rasping. It seemed a long poem. Esther only vaguely listened, her thoughts drifting elsewhere.

> *"The Walrus and the Carpenter*
> *Were walking close at hand;*
> *They wept like anything to see*
> *Such quantities of sand;*
> *'If this were only cleared away,'*
> *They said, 'it* would *be grand!'* "

Why don't the Rats come? Where are the boys? Why doesn't anyone come? Esther's thoughts ran endlessly along the same lines. And sometimes there came another question so dark and bleak that it made her tremble to consider it. *What is going to happen to me?*

> *"Four other Oysters followed them,*
> *And yet another four;*
> *And thick and fast they came at last,*
> *And more, and more, and more –*
> *All hopping through the frothy waves,*
> *And scrambling to the shore . . ."*

Esther felt the old man's grip tighten. His hand was unbearably hot now. His voice trembled with excitement. She looked up at him, but it was as if she wasn't there. She watched the pale candle flame which trembled in her hand. If this goes out, she thought, everything will be in darkness.

> " 'I weep for you,' the Walrus said,
> 'I deeply sympathize.'
> With sobs and tears he sorted out
> Those of the largest size,
> Holding his pocket-handkerchief
> Before his streaming eyes . . ."

Everything in darkness, everything in darkness. She repeated it over and over until she made it her prayer, but it was not a prayer of hope. It was like a lifebelt that stopped her slipping beneath the dark unending waves.

> " 'O Oysters,' said the Carpenter,
> 'You've had a pleasant run!
> Shall we be trotting home again?'
> But answer came there none –
> And this was scarcely odd, because
> They'd eaten every one."

Calmly Mummery said: "Whatever happens, Esther, you must realize I bear you no malice. Moses Mummery bears you no malice. It's just that . . . we are all victims, child. Of nature and time and circumstance. Do you understand?'

Esther shook her head.

"Let us rest here," said Mummery softly. Gently he pulled her down on to the curving side of the pipe. He would not release her.

"Are you hungry, child? I have cheese and bread in my pocket, neatly wrapped up in a handkerchief."

"No."

"Nor me neither. Not a bit hungry. Never am."

"That's because – " Esther checked herself.

Old Man Mummery chuckled. He said. "Blow out your candle, Esther dear. We shall be more comfortable in the dark together. It will be like a cloak over our heads. We shan't have to witness the wickedness of this world."

"No!"

"Blow it out. It will be better. Believe me, a poor old blind man."

"No!"

Mummery, struggling with his free hand, unsheathed his dagger.

"See how its blade shines, Esther dear. I polished it especially. You would not see it shine at all if only you'd blow your candle out."

"Please – no! What are you going to do with me? I haven't done anything to hurt you."

Mummery looked wounded. "I told you. Didn't I say, Esther? Moses Mummery bears you no malice. None. Wait – what was that?"

"What?"

"Hold up your candle, Esther dear. Do you see their wicked eyes? Do you see?"

Esther jerked up her head, flicking the hair from her face. From the direction they had just come, she saw lights. In pairs and singly. Distant. Not reflecting her pale candle.

"Do you see?" rasped Mummery impatiently.

"Yes."

"What are they doing?"

"Coming, Mr Mummery. Coming towards us."

As Esther watched, the lights approached at speed. They were torches. She waved her candle hoping it could be seen. If I had blown it out, she thought, they wouldn't know I was here.

Mummery grew suspicious. He clawed his way to his feet, dragging Esther with him.

"You must be my eyes," he hissed. "We must get away from this place. I sense things. It is a blessing that came when I lost my sight. Now hurry, Esther. Hurry!"

Esther lagged behind as before. This time for a different reason. The flaring torches were getting nearer. She could see heads silhouetted before them.

Old Man Mummery's dagger swung carelessly.

"Hurry, Esther!"

Along the pipe they could hear the march of feet. Then a voice echoed down its length.

"Moses Mummery! Wait for us. We have old times to discuss."

132

"Ghosts!" hissed Mummery, his voice thickening. But Esther recognized the voice at once. It was Man O'Dea.

The rat-catcher turned towards his pursuers, his blind eyes in a face that was proudly raised. Suddenly he jerked Esther to him. She breathed in the scent of violets off his jacket. She felt the dagger's point held against her.

"Who's there?" he demanded.

Tears filled Esther's eyes. Hazily she saw men and women. Their torches surrounded her. She blinked. There was Oonagh. And there were Zachary, Carl, and Frankie too. A laugh came from her as a cough. The boys looked so funny draped in blankets, their hair wet and spiky and the war-paint smudged on their faces. Then the tears silently rolled down her cheeks.

"Who's there I say?"

None of the Rats replied. They stood staring at Mummery in awe, their torches crackling and swirling. Esther could hear Mummery take short breaths. His heart drummed against his brittle rib-cage.

"Ghosts," he hissed again.

"Not ghosts, Mr Mummery." It was Man O'Dea who stepped forward. "Although plenty of ghosts could rise up to curse you. For you laid them in their graves, Mr Mummery. You laid them there."

"I don't know you," rasped Mummery.

"But I know you, Mr Mummery," replied O'Dea. "We all have cause to know you. And we have waited a long time for the day when we would meet up again."

"I don't know you!" replied Mummery more wildly.

"Then I will tell you a story, so you remember," said O'Dea. And when it was absolutely silent, he began.

"Once, deep in the forest, there lived a small community which earned its bread by harvesting the trees and by mining. Each family had its own mine, for in the rock ran veins of gold as thin as pencil lines. I was but a boy then, but the times were good and I never went hungry – "

"What is this?" stormed Mummery. "A fairy tale? A history lesson?"

"Not to us it isn't!" cried a woman.

"Hurry up," said Carl. "I want to know what happened."

"Yes, it makes a good story," admitted O'Dea. "Well, listen and I will go on. One day there came a determined young man to our village. He had a peculiar evil charm that some recognized at once. Behind him rode a gang of armed villains. It was you, Mr Mummery. In your possession was a bogus claim to the land. At once you started demanding rent, as you so quaintly called it, when in fact it was nothing less than an elaborate protection racket."

134

"It was the gold," said Mummery sadly. "It was gold fever."

"You were certainly a man possessed," agreed O'Dea. "Soon rent was not enough. You started seizing the mines themselves. But what good were they without men and women to work them? So you had the forest people rounded up and herded like animals. And like animals you mistreated us, working us till we dropped, starving and beating us, splitting up whole families. Yet you were not the slightest bit concerned. Indeed, Mr Mummery, you appeared to have enjoyed your cruelty."

Esther felt the old man stiffen. The dagger point remained at her side.

"Not enjoyed!" he cried drily. "Never enjoyed. It is something I am driven to do."

"And you do it so well," added O'Dea calmly.

"I don't want to hear any more," growled the old man.

"But you must, Mr Mummery. I've waited forty years to tell you this." And he continued. "About this time the great open-cast mine was made. I say *made* as if it were conjured out of thin air. Many died in its construction, Mr Mummery, including my own parents. But that's a small detail. No more worth a second thought than those buried in the frequent landslides, because we were animals and not worth the cost of properly shoring up the sides. In my head I

135

still see my people, Mr Mummery, filthy and near-naked, swarming over the quarry sides to fetch up the sacks of broken rocks. I was just a child, as I say, but working from six in the morning to six at night in your factory."

Some of the Rats nodded. "We had to break the rocks into powder," said one. "It was a dangerous job."

"Did you have to do that, too?" Carl asked O'Dea.

O'Dea shook his head. "I was put to work in a dark windowless room that in the summertime grew so unbearably hot I would pass out. Those who worked there washed the dust in great pans, and by candlelight searched for the precious grains of gold. It was less dangerous work, I suppose, but by the time I was twelve my sight had completely worn out. It's odd to think we are both blind, Mr Mummery. Although I believe your own sight has naturally worn out with age.

"Then came our escape. You see, Mr Mummery, some of our feelings remained human. Hope was one of them. We rushed the guards, knowing that many would be killed, but many would escape. I myself was led on a piece of string, like an animal, madly scrambling into the night. But of course it was now always night to me."

"I lost my husband that day!" screamed a

woman. "Moses Mummery is to blame!" Instantly other angry voices rose up with hers.

"Hush-hush now," called O'Dea, pacifying the crowd. "See, Mr Mummery holds a knife, and an innocent, and besides I am still telling our story. Quickly, let's pass over the months of endless wandering. Let's arrive at the big house, hungry and tired, wading up its pipes to find a home between the walls and beneath the floors. We knew all about pipes, thanks to you, Mr Mummery, because you kindly taught us how to drain your mines and quarries. What unforeseen luck, and what could be more natural than us becoming the guardians to this underground world. Yet not its human guardians, for we live below the house like rats, and gradually that is what we have come to see ourselves as. Rats. And we have been waiting a long time to cross paths with you again, Mr Mummery. A long time indeed."

"Kill me, then," said Mummery petulantly. He pushed Esther aside. "See, I release the girl. I could have killed her. But now she is gone. So let one good thing be said of Moses Mummery. If you'd feel revenged by striking down an old blind man, then do it. My life is no joy to me. I would prefer to be dead."

"Kill him, O'Dea!" shouted Oonagh. "It's no more than he deserves for what he did to you."

"No," said O'Dea firmly.

"Then let me make it easier for you," said Mummery, some of his old confidence returned. Before anyone could prevent him he lunged towards O'Dea with his knife.

Oonagh screamed shrilly, with every other voice breaking out at the same time. Over the confusion O'Dea's voice soared.

"It's all right," he said. "I'm only scratched."

"Mummery should die!" demanded the crowd but once again O'Dea calmed it. In a voice barely more than a whisper, he said: "Give me a knife similar to that held by Mr Mummery. Or if a blade the same size cannot be found, find me a shorter one."

"Don't be a fool, O'Dea," called Oonagh. "Why take a risk with your own life? Kill him and be done with it."

"Hush there, wild girl," said O'Dea. "Go now and stand away from us. Let no one harm Mr Mummery except myself, for in this we fight as equals."

O'Dea's request was carried out. The Rat people pressed themselves against the pipe's sides, or moved further down its length. A shadow fell between the two men and they themselves grew shadowy. Esther saw a man restrain Oonagh, her body leaning forward like a panting dog on a leash.

For a while the two combatants circled each other, their arms outspread as if for balance. In one hand a knife. The other hand open, fingers wavering like the sensory organs of a sea creature. Neither man made the slightest sound. O'Dea sniffed the air. He could smell violets.

Suddenly Mummery slashed out with his knife. Instinctively O'Dea swept the area before him with his own blade. The scene suggested a dance more than a fight. Sometimes the two men had their backs to each other, pointing their knives at the ring of onlookers. Metal hissed as it sliced the air.

Then, an unbearable stillness. Fingers trembling. The brightness returned to Mummery's eyes. His skin flushed. O'Dea both pale and serious.

As the seconds passed by, both men drew steadily nearer to each other. Mummery smiled confidently. His free hand was like a snake, constantly alive, feeling the air. Then lightly it brushed O'Dea's knife-arm, in a trice gripping it at the elbow with those long elegant fingers. "Ha!" hissed Mummery, his knife-arm swinging out savagely.

"Man!" cried Oonagh.

But Man had managed to crook his elbow, so that in swinging round to face his adversary Mummery pushed himself on to the point of his knife. Mummery gave a dry throaty sigh – but was smiling as he sank to the ground.

Suddenly everyone was talking. Moving.

Shouting. Shrugging. Waving their arms.

Esther and the boys found themselves thrust forward and pressed down by peering faces. They were forced to kneel beside Mummery. He smiled at them. Already his voice had grown faint.

"No one will mourn for me," he whispered. "Nobody. Nor do I much wish them to do so. Tell whoever asks, Moses Mummery was happy to die. Happy to be released for his terrible burden. Tell them he was not always evil. Just a good man who once lost his way . . ."

"He's dead!" cried a man. Others began shouting. The women wept from pure release. Soon they were being shushed. Man O'Dea had also fallen to the ground.

"But he was only scratched!" Oonagh was yelling. "A scratch won't kill him!"

Some men lifted Mummery's dead hand, which still grasped the knife. They sniffed its blade.

"Poison," they agreed.

Oonagh rested O'Dea's head in her lap and stroked the wisps of grey hair.

"Don't you go dying, O'Dea,' she said fiercely through her tears. "Don't you leave me, you old fool."

O'Dea smiled up at her. "What's this, wild girl?" he murmured. "Tears? Not like you, wild girl. You're a growler by nature. Let me die without you scalding me with your tears first."

"Shut up, O'Dea. Think about yourself and getting better."

"Better, wild girl? Why, there's nothing to be getting better for. Moses Mummery is no more. So the world is rid of his kind until the next time. No, wild girl, there are no more claims on my life."

"Me!" sobbed Oonagh. "What about me?"

"You, wild girl? But you're not even a Rat. You're a little pink thing scooped from the water. Squawking then – and you haven't given me much peace since. In my pocket, Oooney-ooney, there's the wallet I go carrying. Take it out. Take it out. It's a clue as to who you really are in this world."

"Don't want it, O'Dea," sobbed Oonagh. "Want you. Want things how they were before. You with your fishing-line and whisky glow. Us alone on our boat . . ."

Despite her words, Oonagh brought out the battered old wallet. Opening it, a piece of yellowed paper fluttered free, folded four times and the folds so delicate they were practically falling apart.

"Don't want these things!" she shouted, throwing aside the wallet. "Want you, O'Dea. Want you."

But Man O'Dea was already dead.

The crowd respectfully drew apart, as Oonagh

rose to her feet. With dignity she passed through it until someone spoke her name. Then she began to run. Madly racing up the pipe, and not once looking back.

A small frowning man approached the children. He told them his name was Jake.

"Please," he said. "Come with me. I can show you the way back to the upper house."

Esther said: "But Oonagh – "

"We will take care of her," said Jake. "She is not a Rat, but we consider her as one of our own."

It was as they followed Jake's flaring torch, that Esther realized she was holding the folded piece of paper that Oonagh had left behind.

Chapter Seventeen

Jake took his leave with some advice.

"Say there has been an accident," he said. "A flash flood in the pipes. Say Mummery was washed away. Tell it as simply as that. His body will eventually turn up in the big lake into which all the drains empty."

They nodded. He stepped back and was gone.

As they stood in the corridor, gazing at the sealed panel, where the door had been, Aphid Dunn briskly turned the corner. She halted, her skirts swaying about her, surprise fermenting into anger as she saw them gathered there.

"There's been an accident," began Zachary breathlessly. "Mr Mummery. Water. Him washed away. Dead."

Apid's rage was wordless. She turned on her

heels and promptly marched back the way she'd come.

The schoolroom: the children newly dressed in warm dry clothes. The boys in Norfolk jackets and scarves, pressing themselves around Esther as she opened the scrap of yellow paper. She did so with care, as if it were a bandage around a painful wound.

"It's a letter!" she exclaimed.

"More like a note," added Zachary.

"Read it to me," begged Carl. "I can't make out some of the words, they're smudged."

Zachary said loftily: "It's rude to read other people's letters." Nevertheless, he didn't prevent Esther from reading it aloud.

" 'This new-born child,' " read Esther in a clear ringing voice, " 'is of no use to me and belongs to whosoever finds it and cares to pay for its upkeep.' "

"The note," said Zachary, "must have been with Oonagh when Man O'Dea found her. Look, here are some little holes at the top. I wouldn't be surprised if it wasn't pinned to her at the time."

"Poor Oonagh," said Esther.

Dinner was tiresome that evening. Aphid was at her most waspish, Miss Pursglove at her dottiest. And Dunn had stirred himself out of his usual stupor to hear the children's rehearsed account of Moses Mummery's death. As he served, Blackhead listened sullenly, being careful not to clatter the crockery in case he missed anything.

"Gone. Dead," said Dunn in amazement. "The chap was here at breakfast, now it is dinner and he is no more. I know we are not supposed to speak ill of the dead, but I for one am relieved. I can't think why he was ever sent for in the first place."

Rounding angrily on her husband, Aphid snapped: "He was sent for on account of the rats. Who were, and still are, plaguing my life here at this house. Making it an utter torment, Mr Dunn!"

"Ah, Aphid. Do you remember our old house in the forest – "

"The draughts. The damp. The wallpaper peeling. Yes. I am trying to forget it still."

"Oh," said Dunn with genuine surprise. "It always struck me as a cosy nest for us, Aphid my love. Things were always as they should be when we lived there."

"Perhaps you should go back," chimed in Carl. He had a potato on his fork, and was nibbling at it in a way he never would have done had the master been head of the table.

"I beg your pardon, young man?" Aphid's voice rose as if she was practising musical scales.

Carl thought this an invitation to expand. He said: "I mean, Mr Dunn has never been happy here. I mean, tonight is the first time in a long while I've seen him happy and that's because Mr Mummery is dead. And most of the servants have left. And everybody bickers and squabbles and gets into bad tempers. If Zachary and Esther could take care of Frankie and me, we would be quite all right liv – "

"Miss Pursglove!" roared Aphid. "Take that ungrateful child's name at once and strike out his meat ration for two weeks. You hear me, Pursglove? Two weeks! Do it now, lady."

"Oh-oh. Yes, Mrs Dunn. Now where's my . . . Ungrateful child, as you say . . . Indeed . . . No more pork or ham for him . . . Ah, here's my l-little booklet . . . Or s-sausages or beef or – "

"Pursglove!" shrieked Mrs Dunn. "What on earth are you fussing for now, lady?" She glared across the table. Miss Pursglove, in her fluster, had emptied the contents of her not insubstantial handbag before her, and was proceeding to rummage through a pile of powder-puffs, keys, handkerchiefs, tickets, letters, sweet-wrappers, spectacles, lucky charms, combs, tablets, ointments and hair-grips.

"My l-little silver pencil," whispered Miss Pursglove, holding a hand to her pale throat. "I appear t-to have misplaced it."

"Misplaced it, Millicent Pursglove! The only

thing you've ever misplaced is your brain. Give me that booklet. Give it here! I will write down the instruction against this impertinent child's name. Blackhead, your pen if you please."

Blackhead smiled. He handed her his pen and bowed. From their side of the table, Zachary and Carl noticed that, when only the top of his head was visible to Mrs Dunn, the smile vanished, to radiantly re-appear as he righted himself again.

Aphid wrote rapidly. Esther took a sly look at the page. The shock of excitement she felt was like two poles of electricity meeting. She saw Zachary and Carl staring across at her in bewilderment. She wanted to tell them at once. Aphid Dunn's writing was exactly the same as that on Oonagh's scrap of paper.

Chapter Eighteen

That night, Oonagh reappeared. Esther felt a soft bump at the foot of her bed. She struggled to sit up.

"Oonagh?" she called gently.

"I had nobody else to talk to," whispered Oonagh through the darkness.

Esther crawled to the foot of the bed and squatted beside the hunched figure.

"Where have you been?"

"In the pipes. Blowing 'em up. Made me feel better. Your heating'll never work now."

Esther reached out and touched her hand. I was like ice.

"Quickly, get into bed beside me. You'll soon warm up."

Wearily Oonagh obeyed. She didn't bother to kick her boots off. They lay close together on the bed's only warm spot, Esther summoning up the courage to speak.

"That piece of paper," she said at last. "The one Man gave you before he d – Before. It must have been pinned to you the day you were discovered. It's a note from your mother, disowning you. It was written by . . . by Aphid Dunn. She is your mother. Dunn is your father."

Oonagh lay still. She said: "In the morning I'll take my knife. First of all I'll kill *her*. Then I'll kill *him*."

"No!" cried Esther. "I'm sure Dunn would never have hurt you. He has always been kind to us in his way. He once told me Aphid couldn't have children. I'm sure he knows nothing about you at all."

"All right," said Oonagh. "So I'll kill her. It doesn't matter to me."

Esther slapped the pillow by Oonagh's head. "Stop being so bloodthirsty. Listen. You must see Dunn. You can save him. His wife is pushing him to the brink and, after all, he is your fa—"

"He is nothing to me!" cried Oonagh, sitting up so a great gulp of cold air entered the bed. "And if that's all you can tell me I'll go back into the pipes. I'll blow them up and drown this house for good."

"Stop, Oonagh! Please stop! Can you ever be happy by roaming about on your own?"

"I was happy enough with O'Dea. He made me laugh."

"And what would he want for you?"

"To be happy. To be free."

"Then why did he give you that note? Why, when he couldn't look after you any more, did he give you proof of your real parents?"

Oonagh fell back, the sheet clutched to her face. When she had stopped shaking, Esther took her hand and led her from the bed. The moonlight reflected in off the snow, revealing a grey skin of dust along the corridors. The clocks had stopped and cold ashes were in the grates. Silently they climbed the stairs. Still leading Oonagh by the hand, Esther pushed open a door. Light came flooding out. Dunn looked up from the floor where he sat surrounded by old toys.

"Hello, Miss Esther," he said sheepishly. "Have you brought a friend to see me? Er, I was just resting. Collecting m'thoughts together. I find it peaceful here."

Esther picked up a few of the toys, clearing a path to him. She squatted down beside him.

"Oonagh *is* a friend, Mr Dunn," she said, suddenly unsure how to break her news. "But there is something else. Mr Dunn, listen," and the words simply tumbled out: "Oonagh is your daughter."

Dunn peered around Esther at Oonagh, who was twiddling her thumbs, her chin tucked awkwardly into her neck. Dunn grinned at Esther stupidly.

"That girl?"

Esther nodded and began to tell the tale. It was a fantastic tale. Dunn was like a child as he listened. He gripped his ankles, occasionally rocking back and forth, giggling inappropriately.

Eventually Esther showed him the four-times-folded piece of paper. Dunn read and reread it.

"See," said Esther. "Written by your wife, Oonagh's mother."

Dunn nodded stiffly. He wiped a tear away on the back of his wrist.

"Yes," he said. "This is Aphid's writing all right. She never did like children. Wanted other things did Aphid."

He looked at Oonagh again.

"So you're mine?" he said softly.

With her chin still tucked into her throat, Oonagh managed a single nod.

Clumsily Dunn clambered to his feet, knocking aside an empty port bottle on the way. He lurched across to Oonagh and embraced her like a bear. Seizing his collar, Oonagh buried her head into his chest.

"A stranger who is my daughter," said Dunn softly. "Lost and found. Something to cherish."

"What will you tell your wife, Mr Dunn?" asked Esther anxiously.

151

"Aphid!" said Dunn, his face suddenly darkening. "Yes, we must have words with our Aphid.'

Chapter Nineteen

In her room, Aphid sat close to the fire, directing furious snake-eyed glances at the ceiling. They were back. The rats – and their night manœuvres had begun.

She tugged her dressing-gown about her. All she desired was a decent night's sleep – just one. But her night had followed its usual pattern. First she'd spent several restless hours in bed following the rats' progress above her, and now here she was again, by the fire, listening to them come and go. She stabbed the burning logs with a poker. "You old fool, Mummery!" she railed. "You couldn't rid me of any of my pests. Not one!"

Suddenly the scratching started again. This time it appeared to be coming from several places at once. Gripping the poker, Aphid got up and paced about the sofa. She stopped and inclined her head. Now it was coming from behind the panelling, and wasn't so much a scratching sound any more but a gentle drumming, as if made by fingers not claws.

Running across to the nearest wall, she rapped it angrily with her bony knuckles. "Shoo! Begone! Did you vermin hear what I say? Get back to your evil-smelling sewers where you belong!"

But the drumming grew steadily louder. It even started up underneath her feet. She paused again to listen, her expression more troubled than angry.

So intense was her concentration that she jumped quite severely when one of her boys gave an abrupt bark. Her boys had learnt to sleep through the usual rat scrabblings, but this was different. In their miniature pyjama suits they came spilling from their baskets, barking, snapping, leaping up at the walls and digging with their claws at the rugs.

"Stop naughty boys! Stop at once!" screeched Aphid.

Neither they nor the commotion stopped. Indeed, the violence of the drumming went on increasing until it sounded like the wild pounding of war-drums. Then even the dogs lost heart, and hid shaking beneath the bed. Their mistress covered her ears. Around her, portraits quaked, mirrors trembled, and just then her bottle of sleeping tablets dropped off the dresser, spilling little white pills over the floor.

Holding her mouth as if she would be sick, Aphid dashed to the door. Throwing it open she froze for a split second, then let out a scream. Facing her was a group of grotesque figures.

Dunn was kneeling on all fours with the brim of his bowler stuffed with peacock feathers. Esther and Oonagh sat astride his back, while the three boys stood or crouched nearby. With toy or imaginary guns the children pointed at Aphid, and every face, even Dunn's, was brightly painted.

"Pow-pow," droned Frankie, firing pretend bullets at Aphid down the barrel of his fingers. "You dead," he smiled.

"This is really quite beyond me," cried Aphid, reeling back into her now silent bedroom. "It's more than a reasonable person can take." Dunn followed her on his hands and knees blowing his lips like a horse.

"Whoa there, Horsey!" said Esther, pulling on his hat brim.

Recklessly Zachary shot his cap gun into the air. "Beware the paleface queen!" he hollered. "She talk with forked tongue."

This set the boys off on a wild whooping dance. They bounced on Aphid's bed and, on closer inspection, the scalps hung about Carl's belt looked remarkably similar to Miss Pursglove's wigs.

Aphid stood over Dunn tapping her foot angrily. "You have quite gone off your head," she informed him. "I used to think you half mad, now you have gone the full way. What on earth is the matter with you, man?"

"Absolutely nothing," replied Dunn cheerfully. "Seems to me perfectly reasonable that a father should enjoy a bit of play with his daughter. Just as it seems to me that you are the one who is mad, dearest Aphid."

"Listen, Dunn, I demand an explanation."

"Why?" asked Dunn. "I've heard all the explanations that are needed." He rose to his feet, meeting Aphid's glare with a look of triumphant resolve. "You're a wicked person, Aphid Dunn. I must have been as blind as your precious Mr Mummery not to see it before. But I see it now. I wants you out of this house first thing in the morning, Aphid, never to return. And don't try to contact me, or ask for any money, for you'll get not a penny. Not one. You've taken too much that isn't yours already."

"But—" Aphid's face dropped. She felt everything she treasured slipping through her fingers. Desperately she tried a different tack. Her voice softened, she said: "Let me put the young ones to bed, dearest. I'll fetch your slippers and a bottle o' your favourite port. You'll be as right as rain after a drop of your favourite tipple."

"What, and give you the chance to poison it on the way? Oh no, madam. I'll not make it that easy for you."

"But—"

Dunn brushed past her without another word. The children had invented a new game. They had found some expensive French talcum powder and were sending smoke signals. Dunn was determined to join in their fun.

Aphid fled from the room and down the stairs. At the bottom she grabbed up a walking-stick from its stand and smashed a mirror and pulverized the ornaments and vases of flowers. She was so angry she could cry. However, her eyes burned, too hot for tears. In this dangerous mood she slunk towards the kitchens.

The dingy kitchen smelt of stewed cabbage and something else besides. Aphid sniffed the air like a rabbit but couldn't place the familiar smell.

The shadowy figure of Blackhead at the mirror didn't turn to acknowledge her as the door slammed.

Aphid gave an infuriated scream. "Blackhead, give me a gun. Give me it now and I'll use it." She threw herself into a chair. "And I don't just mean on vermin either. Look at my rage, I am shaking!"

Still Blackhead continued combing his hair.

The damp silence of the kitchen gradually subdued her. She blinked at the battered travelling bag on the kitchen table. Sliding a candle nearer she made out the initials M.M. printed in gold on the ancient crocodile skin. Idly she delved into it, pulling out fine handkerchiefs and buckled shoes and the occasional fob watch and shaving brush.

"I'd rather you didn't touch that – mam," said Blackhead darkly.

She glared up at him. He appeared different tonight. Older, more sombre. He was not dressed in his usual butler weeds either, but in a dark, old-fashioned suit. Across his chest was a sash the colour of blood; and as he combed his hair he applied liberal dashes of oil to it. When he set the bottle down Aphid squinted up her eyes to read the label. Essence of English Violets, it said.

"I don't think you are aware of how gravely matters stand, Blackhead," she told him. "I have been crossed and I am not a woman who is easily crossed. But I shall fight 'em. You see. With my claws if necessary. You weren't listening, but I said if I had a gun in my hands at this very moment I'd use it – "

"Like you did on the old master?"

"What! What did you say?"

"You 'eard – mam."

"You better watch yourself, Blackhead. Be

careful what you go saying ... How did you know?"

"Oh, you know what it's like – mam? How us servants like a bit of juicy gossip." He smiled mirthlessly. "For a time little else was talked about below stairs."

"Blackhead, I am not in the mood tonight to hear what servants say to each other. It doesn't concern me in the least."

"Oh, don't get me wrong – mam. I ain't got no strong feelings about the old master one way or another. S'pose I wouldn't have become Dunn's right-hand man if he were alive still, so I guess I've got to be grateful in a funny kind o' way. No, Mrs Dunn, you overstepped the mark elsewhere." The youth curtly nodded his head at the bag. "You sent 'im to his death. Mr Mummery. That *was* really out of order, Mrs Dunn. It makes me think I should do something about it."

Aphid spat her words back at once. "What, that disgusting old man? That failed rat-catcher? I had nothing to do with his death."

She watched Blackhead carefully screw the top back on the hair oil. Picking up a candle he crossed to a little cupboard, unlocked it and took something out.

"What on earth do you want that stinking rag for?" she asked, instinctively placing a hand across her mouth and nose.

Blackhead turned to face her. There was a look about him she didn't understand or like. "I'll put it on for you, Mrs Dunn, shall I?"

Before she could answer he pulled the wolf skin over his head. The wolf's fangs hung over his eyes.

"Remove it at once!" demanded Aphid sounding more alarmed than she'd intended. "I mean, that thing must be alive with germs. It's quite unhygienic in a kitchen."

With a leap Blackhead was on the table, crouched on all fours. At that moment he could have been a living wolf.

"Blackhead!" roared Aphid. "Have you and Dunn gone soft in the head together? Why is it that tonight everyone in this house suddenly thinks he is eight years old again?"

She turned to storm out, but Blackhead leapt nimbly in front of her, locking the door.

"Let me out!" she bellowed. "Let me out of this mad house!"

Now Blackhead was dancing before her in a wild, savage way. Aphid took a swipe at him with her hand, but he danced out of reach and across to the kitchen's outer door. There he stopped and began pulling back the bolts.

"Come first light tomorrow you can go," Aphid was saying in the crisp tones of one who was still mistress of the house. "I can't think how you ever rose to such an important position of

trust. Honestly, you are such a schoolboy underneath. I don't know what Dunn was playing at
when he appointed you!"

A blast of icy air silenced her. Blackhead had
cast the door to the gardens fully open. And
there they were, eyes yellow by candle-light,
patiently waiting to be fed.

Aphid gave a scream as the wolf pack poured
in.

Chapter Twenty

It was Carl who saw it first. The dark mass of lithe bodies seething up the grand staircase. An army fallen in behind its leader, Blackhead; but in his wolf-skin disguise the youth looked wildly different from before.

Pressing closely together the pack stared around. It was uneasy at being in the house. No wolf had ever been bound by walls before, nor been in such close proximity to so many humans. The strong scent of man criss-crossed before them causing the fur down their backs to bristle and growls to rise thickly in their throats. Danger was all around but they were hungry enough to be rash; their yellow eyes burning, constantly searching for food.

By this time the other children had stopped their play and were peering through the bannisters alongside Carl. Dunn, leaning heavily on the rail, frowned to himself.

"Well, my little braves," he said. "Are you ready for war?"

They nodded eagerly, holding up their palms.

"Then let us stand prepared."

Thereupon he sent Zachary to fetch his old umbrella – the one that was also a flame-thrower and had lain unused since he and his wife had come to live at the big house. Zachary returned a moment later. "Here you are, Mr Dunn," he panted.

"Let us hope it doesn't fail us," Dunn said with a grim little smile.

The wolves were steadily pouring up the stairs. Waiting until they were directly below him, Dunn stepped out and blocked their way into the upper parts of the house. Blackhead glared at him with furious hatred. Sensing the hate, the wolves growled louder. Dunn didn't flinch.

"Well, boy," he said in a voice quiet but strong. "This is a new turn of events.'

Blackhead scowled. "I ain't no boy," he said. "You best take me serious, Mr Dunn."

"I do. I do. And you take me seriously, Blackhead. Unless you turn around and leave this house I will fry you and your friends. Every last one if necessary, and I'm an expert at scorching wolves with this thing. I promise you, Blackhead, you'll get no further into the house even if I have to stand here all night barring your way."

Blackhead grinned. "Ah, but Mr Dunn, you don't think I have all my wolves with me, do you? Ain't no sense in that. I've used my brain see and sent half up the back stairway."

As he said this Esther threw an uneasy glance to one side. Sharply she drew her breath. Dark shapes were inching towards her down the landing. She saw their eyes. A few moments more and they'd be within pouncing distance.

"Mr Dunn!" she screamed.

Dunn turned, and in turning pulled the trigger on his flame gun. An evil bright glare leapt from the end of the umbrella as well as a terrible crackling roar. Wolves howled and black shapes danced through the fire.

"They're coming up the stairs," reported Zachary.

"There's too many!" called Oonagh.

"All of you – back to the bedroom!" Dunn ordered.

The children needed no second telling. Another blast of fire crackled from Dunn's flame gun. With howls the wolves fell back, enabling Dunn to dash across to join the children, safe from the wolves, behind a locked door. Yet this escape was bought at a terrible price. Fire had caught the curtains and was leaping up to the ceiling; tapestries had become hanging sheets of flame and on the grim portraits heat blisters

164

suddenly erupted, spreading outwards like scabs.

Lazily the first wisps of smoke drifted under the bedroom door. When Frankie saw them he burst into tears.

"Come on, young Frank, none of your drizzlies," smiled Dunn, ruffling his hair. "See, I have a new game to play." And he led Frankie to the fire bell. "See how fast you can turn this, Master Frank. I want to hear you make a lovely big noise and wake everyone up. Think how surprised they'll be."

Naturally enough Frankie was delighted to set the alarm bells clanging throughout the house.

The others raced to the window but found it refused to open. Ice had frozen it to its frame. Without a moment's hesitation, Dunn picked up a chair and hurled it straight through the glass. The children gawped at him, full of admiration, then thrust their heads out into the night.

"Fire! Fire!" shouted Esther and Oonagh.

"Wolf attack!" cried Zachary and Carl.

And Frankie turned the fire bell, laughing at them for sounding so silly.

"Keep going, Master Frank. Keep it rattling along, boy," implored Dunn when Frankie began to complain of feeling tired.

A sickening thud sounded against the bedroom door. Two others followed in quick succession.

"It's the wolves, Mr Dunn," hissed Zachary, nervously pushing his glasses up his nose. "They're trying to break the door down and get in."

"Not while I draw breath they won't," replied Dunn stoutly. "Keep up the cry, you children. We must at least try to warn the other servants. I'll pile up such a heap of furniture behind the door – ha! – it'll take those damn'd wolves a week to dig through it."

And puffing and panting and with sweat beads rolling down his temples, Dunn was as good as his word, throwing up in minutes a mountain of tables, chests and chairs. Beyond it the door thudded every few seconds and the wooden panels gave little yielding groans and began to split. Everyone threw themselves into their alloted task. The children were nearly hoarse from shouting, but they had done well. They heard raised voices throughout the house and, better still, the occasional snap of a musket and a wolf's dying howl.

However, they all froze in their tracks when Blackhead's sinister voice came floating through the key-hole.

"Listen, you dummies," he said, "the flames are bad out here now, so I'll leave you to it. You may think you're off the hook, but you've gone and built yourself a cosy little tomb in there. Ha-ha. The fire's jus' as 'ungry as me wolves. Ain't

166

no skin off my nose who gets fed first. Ta-ta now."

They heard him and his wolf army move off.

As he had intended, Blackhead, with these words, knocked the spirit from those who heard him. Dunn pulled a chair from the top of the barricade and sank down into it. Instinctively the children closed round him, while once more Frankie began to whimper. In the silence they could hear the fire roaring along the landing, consuming everything in its path; and so intense was its heat that window after window went on exploding into the night.

Esther decided that something had to be done. Quietly she rose up, crossed to the broken window and, being careful of jagged edges, leaned out. Below she saw some thin, ragged wolves – the cowardly ones who had run off when fire was first introduced into the fight. Yet, still hungry, they lingered about the house, and seeing the girl they whined eagerly, showing the pink insides of their mouths.

Then Esther turned her gaze towards the upper part of the house and the windows to either side. Seeing all there was to see, she hurried back to Dunn.

"Come on, Mr Dunn," she said. "We have to get out of here." And turning to Oonagh asked: "Will you help me, Oonagh?"

The two girls gently took Dunn's arms as if

he were an old man. Easing him from his chair, they guided him across to the window. Once there, the freezing air appeared to revive him a little. At Esther's insistence he viewed the close-set windows to his right, with the snowy statuary that divided one window from the next.

"If we can crawl along the ledges and over those two statues," Esther explained, "we'll reach the window at the end which belongs to the master's private quarters. It takes you up to his observatory."

"It looks slippy out there, Miss Esther," frowned Dunn. "And I see our friends are gathered below waiting to see if we fall." Then he sighed. "I wish I hadn't been so rash when I broke this darn window." He kicked away as much of the broken glass as he could see sparkling in the carpet. "Get your slippers and socks off quickly now, children," he said. "They'll be no use to you with ice underfoot and climbing to do. Who's ready to go first? Good lad, Zachary. Here take my hand, I'll – "

It was then that it happened. Suddenly the bedroom door dissolved and liquid fire came exploding into the room. The barricade of furniture ignited at once, and the chair, on which just a minute before Dunn had sat surrounded by the children, was consumed by a swirling fireball.

"Quickly now, quickly. But with care!" There

was an edge of panic to Dunn's voice as he lifted out the children.

He himself was last to leave. On the ledge, Frankie was waiting to grip his hand.

"All right now, Frankie, my boy. It's all right," he said. Glancing back, he was appalled to see the thick black smoke billowing from the room. Within moments, fire was rolling out in crackling flares, scorching the walls and spilling orange light down the face of the house.

Underfoot the snow lay bitterly cold, the ice so sharp that Oonagh and Carl left blood trails after them. Further along Zachary had cleared the first group of statues and, unseen, was shouting to Esther the best way to climb over it herself.

Dunn looked down at the wolves milling about like sharks and water sprang to his eyes. "I shall never forgive myself if one of the children falls," he thought. "Never."

Carl, who would not listen or be told anything, climbed recklessly. On the second set of statues he slipped and nearly came to grief, quite unaware of the great burden of guilt he would impose upon Dunn in doing so. Outside the last window, at the corner of the house, the final group of statues was much larger than the previous ones. The children clambered up upon gigantic stone eagles and helmeted centurians, leaving room for Dunn.

"The window's locked, Mr Dunn," Zachary informed him.

"Don't you worry yourself about that, my boy," grinned Dunn. "Hain't tonight seen the rise of a world champion window smasher? Let's see what I can do here."

Slipping off his butler's coat, Dunn wrapped it round his fist, whereupon he simply went on punching at the glass again and again until it shattered. Poor old Dunn waved his reddened knuckles in the air. The glass was thicker than he thought. He reached into the hole, lifted the latch and, climbing through first, carried each bare-footed child past the splintered remains of the window pane.

"Poo!" sniffed Carl, holding his nose.

Even with the house burning down around their ears, Dunn allowed himself a professional frown when he saw the piles of rubbish spilling down the stone steps, dumped, no doubt, by a servant too lazy to carry it out to the rubbish bins below. It took no little effort to navigate a path through the heaps of banana skins and orange peel, rancid rinds of cheeses and stinking bones. But at least there was no sign of the fire, and the reek of rubbish even masked the smell of burning which penetrated every other part of the house.

At the top of the stairs lay the master's observatory. In the darkness, semi-luminous star charts

170

glowed, as did the many antique brass telescopes. Zachary pointed to a circular flight of stairs hidden away at the back of the room; and eventually the group emerged on to a viewing platform built amongst the roofs.

Perhaps they believed the worst part of their ordeal over, for everybody slumped into the snow, panting as if from a long race. Below they could hear the fires raging, and in several places geysers of flame roared up over the very rooftops. Fiercely orange, an unnatural light slid amongst the shadows; and the snow itself was rapidly melting, dripping off gable-ends and gurgling in the gutters. The snow that remained was made dirty by little curly wisps of ash that came floating down from the sky.

"We've rested long enough," said Dunn at length. "We must go on. We'll try to make the southern staircase. It's the furthest away from where the fire began and should be untouched. But we must hurry, the fire's spreading fast."

They nodded and fell in behind him. Cold, scared, some bleeding, and surrounded by a host of dangers, Esther recalled to mind the last occasion they had been on the roof. When the boys had been silly and set the clock striking and she had brushed snow from the stone lions.

In the distance, beyond the shadowy canyon of chimneys through which they were presently passing, she could make out one of her carved lions. It perched on the parapet gazing out over the land towards the forest. Only slowly, as the creature turned to stare at her with lucid yellow eyes, did she realize it was not a lion at all but a living wolf!

"Mr Dunn!" she gasped. "The wolves are in front of us."

"And above us!" came Oonagh's shout at the same time.

Sure enough, there they were amongst the chimneys. The first few were already leaping down and from the shadows came menacing growls.

"Climb up this roof!" bellowed Dunn. "They won't follow, their claws can't grip the slates."

A mad scramble ensued until all six had reached the safety of the roof ridge. From their high position, the children saw that the wolves completely encircled them; while in the distance many more new fires had broken through the top of the house and in number appeared to be multiplying even as they watched.

"Oh please, Mr Dunn," implored Carl. "Use your flame thrower so we can get away from here."

"Move well back then," said Dunn. "You've seen what a terrible weapon this can be."

They inched away along the ridge, crouching down in readiness for the blue searing flame. But when Dunn pressed the trigger, all that happened was a trail of fire that trickled from the barrel and with a hiss extinguished itself in the snow.

"The fuel's all been used," he said.

The children groaned in despair.

"At least the wolves can't reach us if we stay here."

"But the fires soon will," said Oonagh.

"And look," said Zachary pointing. "It's Blackhead."

Immediately their eyes became fixed to the dark, malignant figure dancing in the firelight, twisting and winding his way ever closer, never out of their sight.

"He frightens me," whispered Esther. "He frightens me more than anything."

"Don't go getting yourself alarmed about that one," said Dunn reassuringly. "Remember he's just a boy. Why, he's barely older than Zachary here."

"Shhhh. He's trying to shout something to us," hissed Oonagh.

"Mr Dunn!" called the youth, facing them from a parallel roof-top. "Well, Mr Dunn – sir. I thought I'd seen the last of you tonight. But here we go, meeting up again, and there ain't no door to go hiding behind this time."

"Call off your wolves, boy," retorted Dunn. "Haven't you done all the damage you can possibly do? What can you hope to gain?"

Blackhead regarded him with long and deep disgust. 'I ain't no boy – old man. I keep telling you that. Besides, ain't I proved m'self tonight? Look around you, Mr Dunn. Have a good long look. Not even Moses Mummery could achieve as much."

With a simple gesture he indicated the terrible roof-top scene where some twenty separate blazes were leaping up out of control, and overhead a filthy cloud of smoke blotted out the stars.

The youth allowed himself a proprietary grin. That grin vanished, however, when a voice arose from the shadows and addressed him.

"We have seen enough of your handiwork, Master Blackhead," it said. "More than enough. And we have seen enough of you."

As Blackhead peered amongst the pediments and warped roofs, the voice continued:

"We have rid ourselves of one tyrant, and yet another – smaller one – rises up to fill his place. But not for long."

"It's Jake," said Oonagh excitedly. "It's Jake and the other Rats."

"But where are they?" asked Esther.

At that moment a hundred well-aimed stones came crashing down on the wolves. The stones seemed to rain from the sky itself, falling in a brief but violent shower.

"Show yourselves!" stormed Blackhead.

"Rats are too small to be seen," replied a mocking voice.

"They hide from humans," added a second.

"Besides, your wolves might snap us up in their jaws and shake us lifeless," said a third.

The silence that followed was broken by the rattle of a second barrage of stones. One struck Blackhead on the shoulder just as he was reaching inside his jerkin (making Dunn wonder if he were armed). And those wolves that remained put up a terrible howling. Above half had taken flight, leaving the old die-hards and scarred snouts snarling at Dunn and the children as if they were to blame.

A third barrage and a fourth did much to thin wolf numbers further: some wolves even lay still on the blackened snow, their eyes closed and jaws gaping.

Suddenly Zachary let out a yelp. "Blackhead's turned on his heels. He's running away."

"Hooray!"

"Run back to your mummy, you big baby!" shouted Carl.

Yet as they watched, Blackhead didn't disappear from sight as expected. Instead he made directly for a nearby tower and began to climb.

Zachary held his glasses on to his nose as he watched. "What on earth is he up to?" he said.

"Who cares," shrugged Oonagh, "as long as he's further away from us."

Dunn was less happy. "On that tower he'll be directly above us," he said. "That's bad news if he is armed, and I fear he may be."

"He is! He is!" piped Carl. "Can you see it in his hand? It's a pistol."

Barely had they time to register the fact when a little white cloud of smoke appeared at Blackhead's hand, and, what seemed like seconds later, the slates just below Dunn's boot shattered with a bang. This sudden noise proved a blessing in disguise, for it frightened away the last remaining wolves. As one, Dunn and the children slithered down the roof – but not before another hole had appeared in it and fragments of broken slate were hurtling through the air.

Jake was waiting for them in the shadows at the roof's base. He was most agitated. "Hurry. Please. We are in the greatest of danger, and I don't mean Blackhead. The fire's raging right under us and this section of roof may collapse at any time."

Blackhead shot again and a chunk of chimney-pot dropped at Esther's feet.

"Quickly, follow me," said Jake.

In a low crouching run they snaked through a maze of cupolas, parapets and chimneys. It was obvious that Blackhead couldn't see them for he was shooting wildly now and crying and shouting feeble insults. Finally Jake stopped before the head of a ventilation shaft that resembled those elegant curving ones found on ocean liners.

"The Rats have gone ahead," he said. "We must make haste and follow. Go in. Hurry please. Just climb in feet first and let go."

The ventilation pipe swallowed them rapidly. Dunn, who insisted on leaving last, paused at the final moment, hearing a human howl amongst those of the wolves. He glanced across at the tower. The roof had split open and the tower was consumed by fire. He saw the dark shape of Blackhead for the briefest of moments before the rising flames met and closed over his head. With a push Dunn dropped into darkness.

He discovered, like the others before him, that the ventilation pipe was the most perfect of slides. Bowlerless and shouting, he hurtled down its twisting length. Occasionally the pipe grew incredibly hot, but so fast was he travelling that he barely noticed. Journey's end was as abrupt as it was unexpected.

Splasssssh!

It was undignified for the former butler to thrash about in the water admitting he couldn't swim, but Oonagh and Zachary helped lug him aboard a small rowing boat where the other children sat beaming across at him.

Of those in the boat, only Oonagh and Esther knew where they were. Ahead of them lay Man O'Dea's houseboat. It was towards this the little craft now pointed its prow, propelled by the many Rats in the water. When Dunn remarked upon the injustice of their situation compared to his, Jake simply replied: 'Rats make excellent swimmers, Mr Dunn."

O'Dea's boat practically groaned with so many clambering aboard it: it listed and lay dangerously low (the numbers on board would increase later on when Aphid's bedraggled boys were fished from the water). Then without a moment to lose – the ferocity of the fire and the delicacy of the boat's construction both heavily in mind – the anchor chain was sliced and oars dragged up from below deck. Raising the sail was more of a token action for it had as many holes as can be imagined. In any case there was hardly a breath of wind over the reservoir.

As a team of Rats pulled and grunted at the oars, another team patrolled the gunwhales, pushing away the burning debris that continually drifted alongside. Nor were the children left to be idle, but ran harum-scarum over the vessel, throwing overboard anything that would lighten the load.

"We've sprung a bad leak," called a Rat from below deck.

"I told you Man's boat couldn't hold so many," said Oonagh.

"Pipe ahead!" called the lookout. "We're coming to the main drainage outlet. Stand firm!"

Before them, like a setting moon, appeared a

half circle of light. It was the pipe. Through it water was channelled into the lake beyond. The current grew stronger and, borne upon it, the old house-boat began picking up speed. Jake shouted to the oarsmen to drag their oars back over the gunwhales.

"Coming to now!" bellowed the lookout. A great crack followed his words as the mast and sail struck the top of the pipe and were swept away.

More terrible crashing and creaking arose as the boat was violently buffeted from side to side, with water rushing over it more than once. Suddenly the vessel dipped into a swirling hollow. Water exploded like a firework around its prow. Then with a groan it lurched steeply at an angle, juddered, and was finally still.

It had grounded itself upon the lake's muddy shore.

Gradually the shouting subsided and the clamour of water-fowl died into the distance. Beyond a few bruises, no one was seriously hurt and, as they stood shivering in the mist, the first grey light of day appeared in the East.

Chapter Twenty-One

The children should have been tired, but they weren't. The nightmare was finally over – Mummery, Blackhead and Aphid were gone and there was nothing left in the world to fear. Somehow even the air tasted differently that morning. Who then could think of sleeping?

More practically, Esther turned her attention to Aphid's boys who were shivering in their damp pyjamas. Quickly she undressed them and dried them as best she could. Soon they were looking like ordinary dogs.

"If you ask me," she said without thinking, "it's silly trying to get animals to be like people."

Oonagh grinned at her and, realizing she was surrounded by Rats, Esther raised a hand to her cheek. "Sorry, Jake . . . I mean . . ."

"It's all right," laughed Jake. "Perhaps it is time *we* stopped being animals."

The Rats appeared curiously grey by daylight. But they were much more at their ease. Jake even proved to be something of a clown. He could perform tricks like making coins appear from ears; and when he rolled his eyes the children fell about laughing.

The tomfoolery ended abruptly when Miss Pursglove showed herself at the boat. She was still in her nightdress, but had thrown a man's great-coat over the top, and on her feet were green wellington-boots which also appeared to have been borrowed. Obviously she had slipped over more than once in getting there, for she was encrusted with mud, and her hair was all down and wild.

"Mr Dunn! Mr Dunn!" she hailed from a distance. "A word, if you please, Mr Dunn!"

"Oh-oh. Looks like Ol' Purdy's in a bad mood," said Carl, examining her through a port-hole. "She always shakes her head like that when she's mad."

Dunn raised his eyes to the heavens before going up to greet her.

"Ah, good-day to you, Miss P—"

"Mr Dunn, I have a serious complaint. In fact I have more than one complaint. While you've been out in this – this boat – probably fishing – the house has burnt down around my ears, resulting in the loss of my unique and valuable thimble collection. Furthermore, I was subjected to a dreadful case of manhandling during my escape from the flames and I was almost devoured by a savage wolf, Mr Dunn. It stood glaring at me from less than two hundred feet away. But what does this matter to you, Mr Dunn? – as long as you have had a fine time sailing around in your little boat . . ."

During her tirade, Dunn played his part, shrugging his shoulders and protesting his ignorance; and he agreed how terrible it must have been for dear Miss Pursglove. Suddenly she burst into tears.

"The whole situation since my arrival has been intolerable. I'm afraid I must give in my notice. As of this moment I am no longer of service to your wife. Perhaps you could kindly inform her of my decision when you see her."

Dunn's expression dropped and his voice softened. "I doubt whether I shall see her, Miss Pursglove," he said.

Later on, they walked through the snow to the big house. It was a visit each one dreaded, for in its different way the house had been home to servants, children and Rats alike. Throughout their lives it had stood there vast and unchanging. Now their first sight of it made them stand in silence, and stare. So many of its spires and towers had been swept away. So many familiar landmarks changed. The empty blackened shell was smoking, with yellow flame revealed here and there through vacant windows. Beyond, the wings still burnt fiercely and a thick black trail of smoke rose into the sky. For a good distance around its footings the snow had melted, revealing muddy green lawns strewn with blackened timbers and chunks of wall and statuary.

Sucking in his breath as if making a new resolve, Dunn said: "Do you know what is most odd? I don't feel in the least bit sorry."

"The house had become sick," said Jake. 'It had to die."

Coming nearer still they saw the black heaps of wolves scattered on the ground.

"I could make a necklace from their fangs," said Carl cheerfully.

"You do," said Esther, "and I'll never speak to you again."

The stables, which were undamaged, lay at the heart of all comings and goings. Servants rushed up to Dunn as soon as they saw him and shook his hand. Some openly wept to see him and the children alive and well. Dunn visited the injured, propped-up on bales of straw, and listened to various tales of heroism; and he expressed a genuine amazement at what had been snatched from the flames, when he saw the goods and chattels stacked by the stable door.

"The lads are at the back of the house now, Mr Dunn," one servant informed him. "Of course we can't put the fire out, but we are saving what we can."

Dunn smiled and patted his shoulder.

That evening individual fires still lit up the sky, while in the stables, around a fire of their own, Dunn called a meeting. "We must decide our future," he said. By *our* he meant everybody's, but some servants, who had never guessed the existence of a secret people, regarded the grey-skinned Rats with suspicion. The rumour had spread that the Rats were responsible for the fire in the first place, until Dunn let the truth be known.

"There's no future here, Mr Dunn," said one of the maids.

A lot of servants noisily agreed with her.

"Well, friends, you are free to make your own way," said Dunn. "For my part I will stay. I have always lived around the big house and am too set in my ways to go changing now. Besides – " he winked fondly at the children, "I have a new family to consider."

"So what are you suggesting instead, Mr Dunn?" called somebody from the back.

"That we make the most of what is left us. That we help each other. That we equally suffer hardships for the time being, with the promise of something better to come. We have the stables and other outbuildings – and perhaps we might even patch up parts of the big house. I'm not promising it'll be easy. We'll be cold, the food may run out, and there will be few luxuries, if any at all. But come the spring we could start to rebuild – proper homes of our own this time, taking all the stone we need from the ruins of the big house."

"There's sense in that, Mr Dunn," called a voice.

"You can count me in," cried another; and generally Dunn's plan found favour with the servants.

"What about you, Jake?" asked Dunn turning to his side. "What will you and the Rats do?"

Jake rose to his feet. "My people," he said, "gladly pledge themselves to living here in peace with yours." And he stretched out his arm and shook hands with Dunn.

The boys had fallen asleep in the straw and both Esther and Oonagh were yawning when Dunn settled amongst them.

He put his arms around the two girls, drawing them to him. "Do you really think we can make a go of it?' he asked.

They nodded sleepily.

"In my head I've such plans for us," he said. "I've already got a plot in mind where I can build us a house. It'll be so pleasant. We'll each have our own room. You'd like that, Oonagh, wouldn't you?"

Oonagh sat frowning at the flames. "I don't know if I want a room in a house," she said, after giving the matter lengthy thought. "Do you think that I could have a pipe in the cellar instead?"

Dunn laughed aloud at this. "Why, my dear child," he said. "You can have whatever you wish."

By Andrew Taylor

SNAPSHOT

Smith has a secret – something she doesn't want
Chris to find out – but Chris is determined to
uncover it. How else will he be able to help
her?

DOUBLE EXPOSURE

Something is very wrong with Chris and
Smith's holiday cottage. Rural tranquillity is
shattered by a man who'll stop at nothing to
get what he wants.

NEGATIVE IMAGE

Chris is expecting a quiet weekend, just him
and Smith. But then Chris is kidnapped by
animal liberation fanatics, but they've got the
wrong person . . .

HAIRLINE CRACKS

Sam Lydney's mother has disappeared, and it's
got something to do with the nuclear power
station. But to find his mother, he and Mo
have to work alone.

£2.99 each

Jackaroo
by Cynthia Voigt £3.50

In a distant time and a far-off place there were legends of Jackaroo, the masked hero who rode at night, giving aid to the helpless and money to the destitute. Gwyn the Innkeeper's daughter finds his costume and uses it for her own ends.

The Callender Papers
by Cynthia Voigt £2.99

In the summer of 1894, twelve-year-old Jean Wainwright goes to work for Mr Thiel, cataloguing assorted business and personal papers of his late wife's family. As she works through the papers, she finds clues to a terrible family story. Worse still, Jean realises that the more she learns, the more dangerous her own position becomes.

Tell Me if the Lovers are Losers
by Cynthia Voigt £2.99

Nothing in her boarding school could have prepared Ann Garder for her roommates at college, Niki and Hildy. Their only common interest is volleyball, but this provides a centre for their friendship, and helps to give Ann the strength she needs when tragedy strikes.

The Silver Crown
by Robert O'Brien

"She did not know how late it was, nor how long she had been asleep, when she was awakened by a loud squealing of brakes, a long and frightening screech of tyres. The car stopped so abruptly that she was thrown forward and hit her head on the button that snaps the glove compartment shut ... Ellen saw lying inside a pistol with a long barrel she recognised instantly, and a shimmering green hood with two eyeholes staring vacantly up at her."

Fear gripped Ellen. Who was this Mr Gates? Why had he been so keen to give her a lift? And was that the green hood the robber had worn? This was only the start of her long journey, in which the silver crown played a mysterious part.

"No doubt about the impact of this strange, eerie, absorbing book." *Naomi Lewis*

£3.50

The Chronicles of Narnia
by C. S. Lewis

C. S. Lewis's wit and wisdom, his blend of excitement and adventure with fantasy, have made this magnificent series beloved of many generations of readers. The final book, *The Last Battle*, won the Carnegie Medal for 1956.

Each of the seven titles is a complete story in itself, but all take place in the magical land of Narnia. Guided by the noble Lion Aslan, the children learn that evil and treachery can only be overcome by courage, loyalty and great sacrifice.

The titles, in suggested reading order, are as follows:

The Magician's Nephew
The Lion, the Witch and the Wardrobe
The Horse and His Boy
Prince Caspian
The Voyage of the Dawn Treader
The Silver Chair
The Last Battle

all at £3.50

Order Form

To order direct from the publishers, just make a list of the titles you want and fill in the form below:

Name ....

Address ....

....

....

Send to: Dept 6, HarperCollins Publishers Ltd, Westerhill Road, Bishopbriggs, Glasgow G64 2QT.

Please enclose a cheque or postal order to the value of the cover price, plus:

UK & BFPO: Add £1.00 for the first book, and 25p per copy for each addition book ordered.

Overseas and Eire: Add £2.95 service charge. Books will be sent by surface mail but quotes for airmail despatch will be given on request.

A 24-hour telephone ordering service is avail-able to Visa and Access card holders: 041-772 2281